GROWIN' PAINS

To Ginny Ruth Grover, twelve years in her tiny, dirt-poor hometown of Clemmons, Texas, is twelve years too many. Who, she wonders, would want to live in a dying town strewn with unpainted houses and cowsheds and streaked with red dust? Nobody who wants a future, that's for sure.

Ginny does want a future, as a writer, but her Maw doesn't understand her ambition. Ginny longs for her Paw, who deserted the family three years ago; he would have understood. Yet things slowly start to look up for Ginny once she meets her kindred spirit, the elderly and afflicted Mr. Billy.

Growin' Pains

Growin' Pains

MARY BLOUNT
CHRISTIAN

PUFFIN BOOKS

PUFFIN BOOKS
A Division of Penguin Books USA Inc.
375 Hudson Street   New York, New York 10014
Viking Penguin Inc., 40 West 23rd Street, New York, New York 10010, U.S.A.
Penguin Books Ltd, Harmondsworth, Middlesex, England
Penguin Books Australia Ltd, Ringwood, Victoria, Australia
Penguin Books Canada Limited, 2801 John Street, Markham, Ontario,
Canada L3R 1B4
Penguin Books (N.Z.) Ltd, 182–190 Wairau Road, Auckland 10, New Zealand

First published by Macmillan Publishing Company 1985
Published in Puffin Books 1987

5 7 9 10 8 6

Library of Congress Cataloging in Publication Data
Christian, Mary Blount.   Growin' pains.
Summary: Twelve-year-old Ginny Ruth feels stifled in her small, dying Texas
town, despite her special relationship with physically impaired Mr. Billy.
[1. City and town life—Fiction]   2. Physically
handicapped—Fiction.   3. Texas—Fiction.]   I. Title.
[PZ7.C4528Gw   1987]   [Fic]   86-30246   ISBN 0-14-032234-5

To Beverly Reingold
*Thanks for seeing me
through my own "growin' pains."*

Growin' Pains

ONE

The crusty carpet of snow stretched as far over the sloping hillsides as Ginny Ruth could see. Clemmons looked almost pretty, until she remembered that under that pure white lay the *real* Clemmons—all red dirt and cow dung.

In school the kids had cut out pictures of farms from magazines and pasted them on a big poster. They showed rows and rows of green plants and a man sitting on a tractor under a pretty orange umbrella. The houses were freshly painted, with clusters of multicolored flowers at their windows and walks, and the dirt always looked as black as charcoal and as rich as humus.

Ginny Ruth sighed wearily and shifted her head from the section of window that her warm breath had clouded. She continued to stare at the monochromatic scene.

Clemmons wasn't like those pictures at all. Real farming had died out long ago. It had slowed down when the men went to war and had never picked up again, because the drought hit. The cannery, once the hub of town commerce, was boarded shut, and the cotton gin lay in shambles at the edge of town. The houses were weathered and peeling and most yards neglected. And there was always the dirt the color of rust, the decay that was really Clemmons. This town must be a lesion on an otherwise healthy earth, Ginny Ruth figured.

There were no tractors in Clemmons, either. Instead every able-bodied man, woman, and child bent to the hoe, scratching out enough to feed their own families, if they were lucky. When they were extra lucky, there'd be enough to sell at the side of the highway, should travelers slow down enough on their hurried journeys to more interesting places to notice the crude, hand-lettered signs. Oh, a few of the men got disability pensions, and some of them worked in neighboring towns. But, for the most part, folks made do with what they grew, bartered, or could sell outright.

The women aged early and died young. The men grew stooped and their eyes grew dim with hopeless-ness, unless, like Ginny Ruth's paw, they just upped and left.

One summer's day—during the drought, it was—he hitched down the highway that snaked past the general store and never came back. And, although it had been almost three years since his disappearance when she was nine, Ginny Ruth still found herself staring down the footpath, anticipating his return.

2   "Ginny Ruth"—Maw interrupted her reverie—

"hurry on down to the store now and get those beans in case Mr. Bob decides to close early. He just might, you know, being Christmas Eve and all."

"Yes'm," Ginny Ruth answered grimly. She fought back the disappointment that was welling up inside. Beans—that was a fine howdy-do for Christmas dinner. Still, beans were better than an empty belly.

She couldn't help but feel bitter toward Maw, though. It seemed to Ginny Ruth that she could go into her savings enough to get a small chicken from Mr. Willis up the road. But, no. Maw had to squirrel away every dime she'd ever made at the cannery. Because of its untimely closing, Maw hadn't worked at the cannery since Paw left. But Ginny Ruth was positive that she still had that money tucked away in a savings account at the tiny bank so grandly named First National Bank of Clemmons.

Ginny Ruth pulled her size-too-small coat on over her voile summer dress and slipped her feet into her only shoes, open-toed white sandals that had seen their best days the season before. At least the socks were thick. When she thought of all those pretty dresses and things in that Sears catalog, she wanted to cry.

Paw had called the catalog their "wish book," and the two of them had studied its pages for hours, choosing the things they wished for. But Maw had always clicked her tongue against her teeth, scolding them. "Wishing is just a fool's luxury. If you want something, 3 you got to earn it." She had lectured them piously every time, as if they hadn't a brain between the two of them.

But then Paw would wink at Ginny Ruth and she'd break into a fit of giggles, and the two of them would go right on wishing, even though it made her maw as puffed up as a setting hen.

Ginny Ruth pushed their cabin door closed behind her and stepped gingerly over the snow, trying to place her feet in yesterday's crusty footprints. "Some Christmas," she muttered as she struggled. "If Paw came tramping down this path this very minute, his arms all full of Christmas gifts, now that'd be a real Christmas!"

The wind whipped her hair into her face and stung her eyes. She pulled her coat collar up around her ears and leaned against the wind, trudging forward.

As she passed the Corbetts', Ginny Ruth noticed they'd hung a bower of holly on their front door; and at the Randalls', the sure smell of cornbread drifted through the chimney flue. That meant they'd be having real dressing with their hen tomorrow. Her mouth watered as she considered it enviously.

Thanksgiving hadn't been so bad for her and Maw. Ever since her maw had taken the job of cooking and cleaning at the schoolhouse up on the hill, they both got a good hot meal there on school days. And if there were any leavings they took them home for a real supper. For Thanksgiving there'd been chicken, cornbread, and even some cranberry sauce.

4

But Christmas would be bleak. The school had been closed for the holidays almost a week. And the other folks were too busy making their own meager plans to remember them. Ginny Ruth sighed and wished one more time for laughing, happy-go-lucky Paw.

There hadn't been an awful lot more money when Paw was there. But, with both Paw and Maw working, they had rented a house with electricity and even a butane cooking stove. They'd had enough clothes to warm their backs, and Paw wasn't so stingy with sweet treats. Sometimes he'd take his guitar and go down the road to play.

Maw didn't like that! She said those were the devil's hangouts. But Paw'd come back with his pockets jingling, and they'd go to town and treat themselves to a bunch of stuff—jawbreakers, peppermint sticks, and jelly beans the colors of the rainbow. And thinking the money was evil-earned didn't stop Maw from wearing that little flowered hat Paw bought for her until it plumb wore out. Wore it right into the church, she did.

But Maw was stingy with money. And when Paw took off, she got even stingier.

Ginny Ruth stepped up onto the wooden porch of the general store and tapped the snow from her sandals. Then she pushed into the door, making its bell jangle mightily.

Her toes stung and her cheeks felt icy numb as she backed up to the potbelly stove in the center of the 5 room and hitched up her dress slightly, letting the warm air drift up her legs. The hard pine crackled and popped, its orange flames licking through the grating.

In this store there were always the most glorious smells hovering and drifting in the air. It was almost like enjoying a good meal, just to inhale them, although not nearly so satisfying in the end. She recognized the peppermint right away. But what was that sharp, sweet smell that teased her nostrils today?

Ginny Ruth let her eyes range over the crates and barrels. Pickles, flour, salt, sugar, potatoes—those were always in the store. But today there was a crate with oranges, their skin shiny and reflective, like the glass balls of a Christmas tree.

Fresh fruit like that in the dead of winter must be a miracle! Ginny Ruth picked up one of the oranges and rubbed it against her cheek, closing her eyes and trying to imagine what it would be like to taste an orange again.

"You buyin'?" Bob Ranger's voice cut through to her.

"How much are these here oranges, Mr. Bob?" she asked him.

"Twenty-five cents apiece," he told her.

Lovingly Ginny Ruth replaced it in the crate. Then, with a long sigh, she said, "Fifty cents worth o' dried pintos, please."

She glanced back at the oranges longingly. "Could

I charge me one of them, Mr. Bob?" she asked hopefully. "Paw ought to be getting home for Christmas pretty soon, and he'll settle up with you."

"Sorry, Ginny Ruth. You know I got orders from your maw not to charge anything but staples. You're already on the books for a lot this month, you know. There was them school supplies and—"

She bit her lip. "What if I come over to your place and work it off? I could help Miss Annie with the baby."

"It's cash I need, Ginny Ruth, not busy work. I have to pay for this stuff with cash. I got plenty of bills to pay, too."

Nodding her understanding, she took the sack of beans as Mr. Bob added the new charge next to their name in the ledger on his counter. It was true, she knew: Everybody in Clemmons was poor. It was as if God and the U.S. government had forgotten the town existed. Why, one time she'd looked on a road map of Texas. There were big old dots for places like Houston, Dallas, and San Antonio. But Stallings twelve miles down the road wasn't more than a dust speck on the map. And Clemmons wasn't on the map at all. There were 287 people in Clemmons, but, as far as the world knew, they didn't exist.

Mr. Bob shoved his pencil behind his ear and motioned to her. He reached down into the pork barrel and wrapped a small chunk of salted pork, stuffing it 7 into her bean sack. "Maybe this'll tasty up those beans a mite. Merry Christmas, Ginny Ruth. Tell your maw, too."

"Yes, sir, Mr. Bob. Thank you. And Merry Christmas to you and yours, too."

As Ginny Ruth turned to leave, the door pushed open with a jangle. Miss Marnie stepped inside, patting into place her hair, the color of a muggy dawn. She wore her frayed wool coat with the fox fur collar that had fascinated Ginny Ruth ever since she could remember. It was made to look like a tiny fox with real paws and little button eyes, and it looked as if it were biting its own tail. Ginny Ruth thought the thing must have been dragged home by the cat after putting up a terrible fight, but Miss Marnie wore it with pride.

And well she might. As worn as it was, it was probably the only real fur piece in Clemmons. It had come from grander days, when Clemmons had been in high cotton and Miss Marnie's father had owned the gin. Until she'd sold them off, one by one, her house had been filled with hurricane lamps and compotes and vases and things she said were more than a hundred years old.

Miss Marnie scurried over to the potbelly stove, which was everyone's first stop on a cold day. "Hi do, Ginny Ruth," she greeted. "You haven't been by of late. And I do miss having you read to me, dear." She patted her eyeglass frames. "These old eyes aren't what

8

they used to be, or I'd do it for myself, you understand."

Miss Marnie had the finest collection of books Ginny Ruth had ever seen. And when her own books didn't suit her, Miss Marnie would send right off to the library in Dallas and they'd lend her books in the mail. Ginny Ruth cherished her visits with Miss Marnie. Those books carried her far away from Clemmons, to beautiful places and better times. She would roll their words over her tongue, savoring the feel of them, claiming them for her own.

Ginny Ruth nodded. "Yes'm. I have been mighty busy with home chores of late, Miss Marnie, but I prefer reading to you. Maybe if you asked Maw personal?"

The truth was, while Maw believed that Ginny Ruth's reading just for herself was the next thing to idleness, she thought it was right neighborly for Ginny Ruth to go read to Miss Marnie.

"I'll mention it when I see her at church Sunday," Miss Marnie promised as she made her way to the potato bin.

Ginny Ruth pulled her coat close to her and opened the door to the bleak day again. Clutching the sack of beans and pork, she stepped onto the porch. The wind was picking up and immediately blew away the warm Christmas feeling she'd experienced in the store.

She hated taking charity, even that bit of salted pork. If only Maw weren't so stingy with her savings. Even 9 now she was probably back home, sewing that hand-made dress that would be her Christmas present for Ginny Ruth.

With all those fine dresses in the wish book, Maw was hand-stitching one she'd cut down from her own small wardrobe. Ginny Ruth figured that Maw didn't realize she knew about it. But she'd awakened a few times during the night and seen Maw sitting by the open fireplace that heated their one-room cabin, stitching in its light.

Why couldn't she buy her a dress? Paw had promised her a store-bought dress before he left. Ginny Ruth hated being poor. She hated this town and everything in it. It was ugly and dead. And she knew if she stayed long enough she'd be ugly and dead, too.

TWO

What with her head down against the wind and her hopping from one footprint to the next, Ginny Ruth was paying little attention to what lay ahead. Otherwise she'd have seen him coming.

But she didn't see him. And, before she realized it, she'd run smack dab into Mr. Billy Gaither, knocking the both of them into a snowbank and sending the pintos scattering over the snow like freckles on a pale face.

Of all the luck, she thought grimly. She had managed most of her life to avoid looking or talking to that poor, wretched man—and that wasn't easy in a town that size. Even when Maw had dragged her off to the Gaithers' on a visit, Ginny Ruth had kept her eyes bolted to the flower pattern of their linoleum floor. But now she'd run smack into him in the middle of nowhere, with no place to hide.

Ginny Ruth figured she was about the only young'un in all of Clemmons who'd never made fun of Mr. Billy behind his back. It wasn't that she was more kindhearted than the rest of them, she had to admit. She 11 just didn't like to think about him one way or the other.

Mr. Billy had made it through World War I without a scratch. But after he got home he was kicked in the head by a cow he was milking. Now he shook all over, and his speech was barely audible. His hands trembled violently, his arms jerked in their sockets, and even his head jumped spasmodically almost all the time, the same way a dead chicken kept on jumping, long after its neck had been wrung. It made Ginny Ruth sick to her stomach to think about it.

Most of the grown-ups carried on real conversations with Mr. Billy, but that meant concentrating hard on what he was saying, watching the movement of his lips. And Ginny Ruth couldn't for the life of her bring herself to look at him close enough for that. He always had spittle on his chin and at the corners of his mouth. And his eyes were moist looking, as if they were going to liquefy and spill from their sockets any minute.

Maybe she had more trouble dealing with Mr. Billy than most folks, but she reckoned it was for a pretty good reason. Something had happened after one particularly hellfire-and-damnation sermon delivered by the resident preacher.

The Reverend Amos Trowbridge had been talking about the sins of their fathers being visited upon them. The church had been extra hot, adding special emphasis to his dire predictions. The air, heavy with sweat, had been only slightly circulated by the palmetto
12 fans, compliments of Dodson's Funeral Home. The

handful of old men had punctuated each of the preacher's sentences with hearty amens, each trying to make the Lord hear his own voice above all the others'.

Ginny Ruth had squirmed uncomfortably between Paw and Maw, all the time watching the bench in front of her tremble with Mr. Billy's movements. After the service her folks had stopped in the shade of the pin oaks of the churchyard, fanning themselves and commenting on the awesome sermon with others in the "flock."

When the Gaithers had come up to them, Ginny Ruth had shrunk behind her maw's skirt. She'd refused to so much as nod to them, despite the sharp look from Maw.

Later, as they walked the footpath home, Ginny Ruth had figured to impress Maw with the fact that she'd been paying the strictest attention to the reverend's words and said, "I wonder what terrible sin Mr. Billy has committed to be visited upon by such wrath."

Paw had laughed heartily. But Maw had pulled a switch from a nearby bush and nettled her legs until they throbbed as if stung by a thousand bees. She'd given Paw a real what-for, too, she had.

It wasn't long afterward that Paw took off for good. Not that Ginny Ruth really could honestly blame Mr. Billy for it, she realized. It was Maw's uncompromising ways.

Of course, without even a fare-you-well note from Paw, there wasn't any proof of that. But Ginny Ruth   13 had no doubt that it was Maw's haranguing and fussing every time Paw wanted to have a little bit of fun.

Anyway, she couldn't look at Mr. Billy without thinking of her paw. It didn't seem fair. Why couldn't Mr. Billy have gone away instead? It seemed to Ginny Ruth that everybody, including his wife, would be a whole lot better off.

But now there she was, face to face with Mr. Billy, the both of them sprawled in the snow. He seemed a bit bewildered by it all. She finally forced herself to speak. "Are you hurt, Mr. Billy? I'm awful sorry. I just wasn't watching."

He mumbled something that she couldn't understand and tried to pluck a bean from the snow. His hands shook like fish flopping on the bank. Ginny Ruth felt the familiar nausea rising to her throat. She knew he'd never make it to the bag with a single bean. And she noted with dismay that the wet snow had eaten a hole in her sack.

Ginny Ruth gathered beans swiftly, stuffing them in her coat pockets. She wrapped the sack around the precious salt pork and put it in her pocket, too.

Mr. Billy still muttered to her, and she strained to understand, trying hard not to stare at the spittle on his chin. He'd managed to pluck one bean from the snow and tried to hand it to her. She swallowed hard once, then held her hand out, palm up, and waited miserably as he tried several times to put the single 14 bean in her hand.

Ginny Ruth ached to grab it herself and run. But she tried to remember what Maw had said that day of the fearful switching: "A man's got his pride, Ginny Ruth. Even a man as tormented as Mr. Billy wants to do for himself what he can."

So Ginny Ruth waited, forcing herself to look into his face as he succeeded at last in getting the bean into her hand. For the first time Ginny Ruth realized that the photograph of the handsome soldier in the Gaithers' living room was Mr. Billy. Maw said Mr. Billy wasn't all that old now, but he must be an old man— nearly fifty.

Yes, it was the same man, but he was trapped inside a twisted, quaking prison. There was the same determined strength in the eyes, and that surprised her. It scared her a little, too. Suddenly she felt she had to get away.

Ginny Ruth helped Mr. Billy to his feet, aware of his trembling even through the heavy coat sleeves. She brushed the snow from his coat as best she could.

Making herself look straight into his eyes again, she said, "Merry Christmas!" She smiled, more from her own boldness than from the spirit of it.

He mumbled something to her, and she figured he was returning her greeting. "Thank you, and to your wife," she added before hurrying down the path.

She thought she had detected a look of satisfaction, maybe even happiness, in those liquid blue eyes. That puzzled her even more.

Ginny Ruth tried to shrug off the encounter and hurried home. She told Maw the whole episode as she emptied beans from her coat pockets, swelling with pride as she remembered her boldness. "I told him Merry Christmas, Maw," she said, half expecting a bit of praise.

"And well you should," Maw replied without a hint of appreciation. She washed the beans and put them on to soak a bit.

"That was a fine thing for Mr. Bob to include that salt pork with the price of the beans," Maw said. "I'll put them on to cook while we sleep tonight and we'll have ourselves some tasty beans tomorrow."

Ginny Ruth felt the bitterness creep over her again. "I bet even Mr. Billy will have a hen for Christmas."

"It's entirely possible," Maw said. "Folks have what they can."

"We don't!" Ginny Ruth snapped.

"You ain't gonna start about a hen again, are you?" Maw muttered. "You need to remember that work at the school is only nine months. But we have to eat twelve months. If we portion it—"

"Beans!" Ginny Ruth moaned. "What kind of Christmas is that? We aren't having Christmas! We haven't had a Christmas since Paw left—not since I was ten years old! God would be awful displeased at the way we celebrate His son's birth, I bet!"

Maw's eyebrows knitted and her face darkened. 16 "Ginny Ruth! You talk like the devil himself! Shame!

Why, you know it's a sin to turn the Lord's birthday into an excuse for your own gluttony and greed!"

Ginny Ruth squared her jaw stubbornly. Her thoughts churned and spun like a dust devil. What made Maw such an all-fired expert on what was and wasn't sin? Maw was always ready to cast that first stone.

"If you weren't so stingy with your cannery savings!" Ginny Ruth stormed at Maw. Even as she spoke she remembered once seeing a fly frantically fighting to free itself from a honey spill. She realized that her own efforts were just as futile. Still she felt compelled to try.

"Why couldn't we just once have a *real* Christmas dinner? Why couldn't I just once have a store-bought dress? Paw promised me one. If Paw were here—"

The redness of rage flooded Maw's face. Her body looked stone hard, as if she were willing it to become motionless, to restrain from striking out at Ginny Ruth.

"Well, your paw ain't here! So just set your mind to that fact, missy!" Her words took on a serpentlike hiss. "And I ain't dibbling out what little we got on no silly frills."

Ginny Ruth wailed, "Oh, Maw. Maw, why?" Her voice faded to a whimper.

Maw took a deep breath, squeezing her eyes shut a moment. When she opened them again, she pulled the Bible from the mantel as if the scene had never happened. "Find the Christmas story," she said, softer now.

She hung the beans on the hook in the fireplace, then eased into the scarred rocking chair. She closed her eyes, nodding as the unpainted floorboards creaked rhythmically beneath her.

With a sigh of submission, Ginny Ruth thumbed through the book until she found St. Luke's version, her personal favorite, then sat cross-legged on the floor at Maw's feet. There was no use arguing with Maw. She might as well enjoy what she could of the season.

It had been a tradition in their family as long as Ginny Ruth could remember to read the Christmas story from their Bible. It was a tradition that Paw only endured but Ginny Ruth actually enjoyed for the peace of mind it brought her. She closed her eyes and listened as once again the images of the Holy Family, the Wise Men, and the shepherds drifted lazily before her.

When Maw had finished reading, Ginny Ruth replaced the Bible. With peace and forgiveness in her heart, she kissed Maw lightly on the forehead, then slipped off her dress.

Sliding under the quilt in her petticoat, she felt beneath her pillow to see if the seeds she'd gathered and dried last summer were still there in their envelope. They were from wildflowers that grew in the stand of pine trees close by. Ginny Ruth had visions of their cabin adorned with clusters of the multicolored flowers, just like those in the magazine pictures.

In Clemmons, though, the same iron in the dirt that turned the earth so red played odd tricks on the flowers. It turned most pink flowers a bluish hue. And it gave a smoky blue haze to green. The flowers, like the town, could never really be what she wanted them to be.

Ginny Ruth closed her eyes, pretending to drift right off to sleep. Maw would probably have a bit more hemming to do on the dress. Faded and sad as it seemed to Ginny Ruth, she realized it would be her only gift.

The aroma of the pork bubbling with the beans teased her nose now as the present faded away and she melted in her dreams to a happier time, when the cabin rang with Paw's laughter. "Quit your jawing at us, Maw!" he'd chide. "Don't you see that life can be fun if you just let it? Don't work so hard at making us miserable. Whatever happened to that happy young thing I married?" He'd wink broadly at Ginny Ruth, and she'd giggle hysterically, to Maw's dismay and anger.

Ginny Ruth didn't know how long she'd been asleep, but the sudden sound of crunching snow outside awakened her. She glanced over and saw that Maw was asleep.

With her quilt wrapped around her, Ginny Ruth crept to the frosted window and peered out. The snow reflected the moon so brightly that she could see the figure of a man.

"Paw," she breathed. "It's Paw come back." Her heart pounded in her chest.

But even as she said it she realized that he could   19

not be Paw. That man's body shook and jerked spasmodically while he moved about the tiny pine tree that grew by their footpath.

Ever since Paw left she'd had this big pit in her. But now, seeing Mr. Billy out there when it should have been Paw, it was as if red-hot coals had been dumped in that empty spot. She trembled from fury at Mr. Billy. Why wasn't it Paw? Why did Maw have to drive Paw away?

What was Mr. Billy doing outside their cabin on Christmas Eve? He was bending over a little sack of some kind. But what was in it?

Curiosity replaced her resentment. The walk from his house to theirs was long and chilling for anyone at night. But for Mr. Billy it must have been particularly torturous. Carefully she wiped a bit of frost from the window to get a clearer look at him.

Squinting through the mist, she watched Mr. Billy struggle to hang something on one of the tree limbs. In the moonlight she saw it was a peppermint cane. Then under the tree he set two shiny oranges like the ones she'd seen at the store. Her nostrils twitched with the sweet memory of their fragrance.

Tears spilled down Ginny Ruth's cheeks as she watched him make his way slowly back down the footpath, his body swaying, fighting him at each step.

"Mr. Billy," she whispered as his twisted, trembling silhouette disappeared into the night shadows, "I just 20 never noticed before what a truly beautiful man you are. Purely you are that."

She stood, staring at the tree with its gifts. The cane gleamed in the moonlight, dancing as the wind blew the limb. A rabbit hopped past, paused briefly to investigate, then moved on.

Ginny Ruth tiptoed back to bed, pulling out the little notebook she kept hidden away. The Reverend Trowbridge, who doubled as the schoolteacher, was annoyed by her tendency to write poems in the margins of her arithmetic papers. So he had given her the little notebook to write in. Regardless of his reason, she was glad to have that secret place for her thoughts.

Hastily she scratched the words that poured from her heart to her hand.

> *Crippled man and half-growed girl,*
> *We're the same, aren't we?*
> *Trapped in unloved bodies,*
> *We both need to be free.*

She whispered the words, listening to their rhythm. She frowned, crossing out "growed" and correcting it to "grown."

The reverend had told her she didn't write like any other twelve-year-old girl he knew. She hoped that was good. Ginny Ruth read it once more, running her fingers over the indentations the pencil had made on the paper before closing the notebook and slipping it under her bed.

She glanced over to assure herself that Maw was still asleep. She'd never understand Ginny Ruth's poetry, any more than she understood her need to write it. "If you are aching for something to do, there are plenty of chores," Maw would say. Although Maw was no more than thirty-four, she seemed ancient in her ways.

Ginny Ruth drifted into a contented sleep, awaking only as Maw stoked the fire back to life the next morning. She twitched with her surprise but waited until Maw had acknowledged her gift of seeds and she had reluctantly modeled the "new" dress that hung limply from her small frame. If she didn't grow at a faster rate, that dress would be no more than a worn-out rag by the time it fit her. How typical of Maw, Ginny Ruth thought, to be so "practical."

Finally, when she could no longer contain her excitement, Ginny Ruth led Maw to the window and cleared a spot of frost away with her hand.

"Christmas has arrived in all its glory, Maw. Look!" she said, pointing toward the decorated tree outside. As if on signal, the wind set the peppermint stick dancing on the frail limb.

Maw's face tightened into a pinched frown. "Is your paw lurking around out there? That's just the sort of thing he'd come up with!"

Ginny Ruth felt herself go limp with disappointment at Maw's reaction.

"No, Maw, Paw ain't here," Ginny Ruth almost whispered.

Maw's expression relaxed a bit. "Then who? Who on earth would bring anything to us?" she asked.

Ginny Ruth opened her mouth to reply. But she remembered that Mr. Billy came when he thought nobody would see him. Instead she answered, "It's just like in the Bible, ain't it, Maw? A wise man brought the gifts. Yes'm, a beautiful, wise man."

She smiled contentedly. Let Maw argue with the Bible, she thought with no small satisfaction. As for Mr. Billy's visit, she vowed to herself that it would remain a secret, Mr. Billy's and hers.

THREE

Maw declined to indulge in the surprise treats and warned Ginny Ruth that she'd only be disappointed if she expected any more such luxury in poverty-ridden Clemmons. Undaunted, Ginny Ruth tried to make the treats last her a few days, reluctantly swallowing the last delicious orange section before it shriveled from old age.

The weather had turned even more sour than usual, and icy rain kept them cabin-bound for the most part. Ginny Ruth howled her protests each time Maw sent her out to fetch water from the deep well or bring in another few split logs for the fireplace although, deep inside, she was grateful for even those chilling escapes from the small cabin they'd lived in since Paw's departure.

Until the cotton gin had shut down and their income had dwindled, they had lived in a real house a quarter mile down the road. Paw had worked at the cotton gin. He had had longer hours than Maw, who had worked at the cannery only when Ginny Ruth was in school.

If only Paw could have stayed on, he would have found some way to make ends meet. Paw could charm the birds right out of the trees, then turn around and sell them back their own nests!

Whenever the rain slackened, Maw went down to sit a spell with Mrs. Corbett, who was ailing with the flu, or to join the Ladies' Circle, which she couldn't do when school was in session. Ginny Ruth took those opportunities to pull out her secret notebook. She recopied her poem and entitled it "Kindred Spirits."

On one of Maw's visits to the Corbetts, who owned a dairy cow and sold their excess milk, she promised to bring back a container of fresh milk. She drafted Ginny Ruth to fetch a package of barley and a few soup bones from Bob Ranger's store. If the carrots and potatoes hadn't gone soft, she was to get enough to fill out the soup. Their own vegetable patch hadn't yielded much for canning that year, and they depended on the store more than ever.

Before she left for the store, Ginny Ruth impulsively made an extra copy of the poem and drew a border of little flowers around it. On her way to the store, she stopped at the post office boxes, located in one wall of the Drummond Feed and Hardware store. She folded the poem and slipped it through the slot to Mr. Billy's box.

Ginny Ruth regretted her bold move almost immediately, fearing what Mr. Billy might think. The very next day she went back to his box, hoping to 25 retrieve it. She poked her eye as close to the glass front as she could and saw that Mr. Billy's box was empty.

"Hi do, Ginny Ruth," Mr. Drummond greeted, startling her into a jump. "This over here is your box, girl, and it appears you done got some mail in it, too."

"It ain't the time of the month for our light bill," Ginny Ruth observed aloud. "And we don't get nothing else." Her heart thumped against her rib cage. Maybe it was a letter from Paw, telling her he was coming home.

"I ain't got the box key," Ginny Ruth said. "Do you reckon you could pass it around to me?"

Mr. Drummond disappeared around the wall and in a minute reappeared with a newspaper. Puzzled, Ginny Ruth accepted it, turning it over in her hands, thanking him. She retired to a corner near the front door to examine the unexpected mail.

It was a weekly newspaper with a county-wide circulation. One section had been circled crudely in red. "The *County Times-Caller* regularly invites its readers to submit poems, for which it will pay twenty-five cents per column inch for any poem published on this page." A first-class stamp was clipped to the paper.

In the upper right-hand corner of the newspaper was the mailing label. It was addressed to Mr. Billy Gaither. He must have put that in her box. She flushed with relief. That meant he liked her poem! She didn't know what a "column inch" was, but getting paid for a poem that just spilled free from the heart was a possibility she hadn't even considered.

As she hurried home later with the groceries, her thoughts whirled around the prospects. She wouldn't—couldn't—send the newspaper "Kindred Spirits." That was their poem, their special poem. It was much too personal. She scoured her secret notebook until she found just the right one.

Carefully she copied it, adding her name, age, and post-office-box number. She folded the paper, blank side out, and addressed it to the newspaper editor. Ginny Ruth got her school paste off the mantel and dabbed some along the edges, closing it. She licked the stamp and applied it to the address side, then hugged it to her. "Oh, please, please," she whispered.

Ginny Ruth tucked it under her pillow, where it stayed until she next went into town on errands for Maw. Now all she could do was wait. She figured she was pretty good at that.

The New Year passed unheralded, except for Ginny Ruth's ceremonious replacement of the old 1947 calendar with a 1948 one from Drummond's store that had a white-faced heifer on it.

The clang of the bell in the schoolyard summoned the children back on the following day. To the accompaniment of a few late-rising roosters, Ginny Ruth and Maw carefully picked their way up the sloping road 27 that was more ice than snow after the recent rains.

The red brick schoolhouse sat on the white hill. It reminded Ginny Ruth of the cherry-topped sundae on the drugstore menu.

Across the road from the school was a weather-stained frame house with an open porch that was entirely void of such Clemmons conveniences— necessities, really—as rocking chairs or swings. It seemed as bleak and somber as the couple who lived there.

Even in the summers they never sought the few pleasures of country life that other Clemmons folks cherished, such as taking their ease after supper to observe the setting sun and nod to the few passersby. They held to the belief that idleness was a tool of the devil, and they were not about to give old Satan any help, Ginny Ruth figured.

Instead the old couple were usually seen in the summer dusk fighting the nettles that choked their vegetable patch. In the winter they could be found scraping the snow from their front yard as if it were somehow unnatural for the season and vicinity.

"Watch your step, missy," Maw warned Ginny Ruth. But the clipped tone with which she spoke let Ginny Ruth know that she was more concerned with her own pride than with Ginny Ruth's safety on the glassy snow. It was the umpteenth time Ginny Ruth had been told indirectly to hold her head high and not look in the direction of that gravestone-colored house.

"Ain't you even curious to see how they're faring?" Ginny Ruth asked. But she knew Maw's answer by heart; it was almost routine by now.

"It's none of our business how the Simmses are faring," Maw replied, her chin forward with the stubbornness Ginny Ruth hated and respected almost simultaneously.

Maw said "the Simmses" as if they were strangers, as if she hadn't been born with that name herself. "But I wonder about 'em, Maw," Ginny Ruth persisted. "They are my grandpa and grandma, aren't they?"

"You don't have no grandparents. And I don't have no parents," Maw insisted. "The sooner you come to grips with that fact, missy, the better off you'll be."

It was the same story Maw always told. Ginny Ruth had actually believed she had no grandparents until she started school six years ago.

It was then that the older children shared that juicy tidbit with her, the story their folks had whispered and no doubt embellished among themselves for years.

The story was that Maw had defied her folks' wishes by marrying the handsome and "ne'er-do-well" young drifter, Marcum Grover. He had come in looking for work at the gin mill and "turned her head" from the local boys. They'd run off to the county seat and married. Her folks had refused to relinquish her hope chest of linens and knickknacks, saying that a courthouse wedding with a justice of the peace officiating wasn't binding as far as they and God were concerned.

Words had passed between them hot and heavy. Maw had stormed from the house then and there. They'd never spoken again, although Ginny Ruth reckoned it was more habit and pride now than real anger.

She sneaked a quick peek at the strong, straight back of Mrs. Simms—it was hard to think of her as Grandmaw. The old woman stood stiffly throwing corn feed to the squawking, flapping chickens that crowded around her feet in the front yard.

Mr. Simms was splitting a piece of firewood, although he swung the axe with too little vigor for the task. Those two were already older than a lot of folks lived to be in Clemmons. Ginny Ruth figured part of it had to be their sheer stubbornness, the same stubbornness that Maw showed on so many occasions. If pride and stubbornness were gold, they'd be rich, Paw had said many times. Ginny Ruth reckoned he'd been right on that.

"Keep your eyes forward," Maw scolded her. "And walk with some pride, do you hear, missy?"

Ginny Ruth and Maw stepped over the cattle guard that discouraged cows from grazing in the schoolyard and hurried past the rusting seesaw and swing set to the double oak doors. They stepped inside. It felt even colder inside than out.

The Reverend Trowbridge, who was principal as well as teacher of the eight grades available in Clemmons, unlocked the school each morning and rang the summoning bell. But it never occurred to him to build the fires, it seemed. That chore was saved for the first arrival, which usually meant Ginny Ruth, since Maw headed straight for the kitchen and her own chores.

Only one classroom was used now, although the school had enough rooms for the grades to meet separately. It had been built in grander days, when it appeared that Clemmons was an up-and-coming town. The remaining four grades required for graduation were available only in Stallings. The few Clemmons "graduates" who went on to finish were picked up by a school bus in front of the general store. Because the bus made stops in rural communities all over the county, the students had to be ready before dawn. Truancy seemed more attractive to most.

The reverend moved around the room from one student to another, seeing that each was busy at some appropriate study. He had taken over the chore when it became impossible to keep teachers in Clemmons. He did have a lot more success than the frail young women who had tried to keep some of the bigger students under control. At times he was known to break into one of his sermons, better suited for Sunday mornings, and that seemed almost as effective as the big paddle that leaned in the front corner.

Actually that was a new paddle. Lester Moore, who had entertained the old paddle more than anyone in the history of Clemmons School, had fed the last one 31 to the potbelly stove before the Thanksgiving holidays. He'd said it didn't seem right that his was the only seat ever warmed by it.

In addition to the classrooms, there was a gymnasium/cafeteria and a kitchen with a butane stove and an electric ice box that stored food for days. There were electric lights, of course. But it was easier on the sparse school budget to heat with firewood.

Ginny Ruth grabbed a few pieces of wood from the stockpile at the back of the room and poked them into the stove. She crumpled paper and threw it in, then touched it with a lighted match.

It crackled and popped, releasing the scent of pine sap, then settled gradually to a glow. The outskirts of the room remained cold all day, especially next to the high, wide windows, so most students gathered in the warmer spots close to the stove. There was little truancy in the winter; children had fewer chores at home then, and they were grateful for the warmth of the potbelly stove around which school life centered.

The Reverend Trowbridge was writing several class assignments on the chalkboard when Ginny Ruth finished building the fire. So she backed up to the fire to harvest the fruit of her labors in the form of a warm backside.

There was a shuffle of feet in the hall outside as the others began arriving. The bitter smell that preceded him told Ginny Ruth that Lester Moore was the first. As if Lester didn't have enough problems fitting in with the others, his mother hung an asafetida bag around his neck the first cold spell. And, although its odor became ranker and its yellow brown stain more offensive, he was not allowed to remove it until spring.

Lester was fourteen and two grades behind in school. He should already have graduated to Stallings. But his father wouldn't let him quit. Mr. Moore couldn't read or write, and he was determined that his son fare better.

The reverend agreed to try to teach Lester as long as he showed up and didn't cause any trouble in class. Ginny Ruth figured the only way Lester was ever going to get out was in a schoolhouse fire. Even then, he might not know enough to leave.

Lester lumbered in and squeezed himself into the small desk, winking broadly at Ginny Ruth. She blushed, embarrassed that he chose her, of all people, to be sweet on. Ginny Ruth looked away, pretending she didn't see him.

There was a swirl of activity as the four Davis sisters giggled and bounced their way into the schoolroom. The Davises were responsible for a large percentage of the enrollment. Ginny Ruth envied them their good humor in the face of Clemmons life. They seemed always to have some private joke among them, and Ginny Ruth loved it when they allowed her to become a part of it. They reminded her of the fun she and Paw had had together.

Even Daniel was of special good humor, considering her name. Her father had tired of waiting for a son, 33 and when she was born, he'd named her Daniel Junior.

The girls swarmed around Ginny Ruth like a gaggle of geese. "Ginny Ruth!" Cyrilla squealed. "It's been forever since we saw you. Can you stay the night with us on Friday?"

"I'll ask Maw," Ginny Ruth promised. Her heart did a small jig. There was never a dull moment with the Davis girls, and she stayed over with them whenever she had the chance.

The Reverend Trowbridge called the class to order as the last of the students straggled in and hung their wraps on the hooks at the back of the room.

"Ginny Ruth," he said as she slid behind her desk, "Miss Marnie gave this to me at the prayer meeting last night and asked that I deliver it to you personally." He shoved a leatherbound book of poetry toward her. He smiled slightly.

Ginny Ruth took the volume, inhaling its leathery smell and feeling its cool smoothness. She returned his smile, fully realizing Miss Marnie's scheme. Maw would probably fret over the care of the book and insist on Ginny Ruth's taking it back as soon as she'd read it, thus assuring a visit soon.

Cyrilla leaned over and made a face out of the reverend's view. "Why do you put up with that crazy old lady anyway?" she whispered. "Don't she scare you none with all that weird talk?"

Ginny Ruth pretended not to hear. Cyrilla was her 34 best friend in the whole world, but they weren't the least bit alike when it came right down to it. Cyrilla thought reading was a skill to learn just so she could pore over the comic books and the few magazines at the drugstore.

Not that those magazines hadn't given them some fascinating things to think about, especially all those stories that came under titles like "On Becoming a Woman" and "What Being a Woman Means." It all sounded a lot nicer coming from the magazines than from Alpha and Beta, Cyrilla's older sisters. Ginny Ruth and Cyrilla had managed to glean answers to quite a few puzzlements from those magazines before Mr. Booker had chased them away and threatened to tell their mothers.

But Cyrilla just didn't know what a magical place Miss Marnie's library was. As for Miss Marnie's being crazy, well, she wasn't at all. She behaved quite normally most of the time. It was only when she prepared for Jake that she seemed to have trouble with reality.

Long before Ginny Ruth was born, Miss Marnie had been married. Her husband, Jake, had worked in a sawmill that could be reached more easily from the community of Iota, about three miles away. But he had cut his own path through the tangled underbrush of the piney woods that ended at the north wall of their two-story house.

In the long summers he easily had made his way back and forth. But as the winters claimed the light earlier and earlier, it had been his habit to carry a small 35 lantern to trace his final steps home. Miss Marnie had always lit a lamp in the window to serve as his beacon.

One evening Miss Marnie had been late getting home from "doing the Lord's work," as she put it. It had been dark already when she reached home and lit the lamp. Jake had never come home.

Some said he tired of the harsh life and took off in another direction to build himself a new life. Others, admitting that the dense forest had claimed more than one person who haplessly strayed no more than a foot from the path, said he lost his way home.

Miss Marnie continued to light the lamp in her window every night. She still believed that Jake would return.

The reverend passed out arithmetic papers for the different grades to work on while he sat up front, studying his notes for the upcoming Sunday service. He made Ginny Ruth sit by Lester and help him, much to her chagrin.

Ginny Ruth was grateful when the reverend finally got a whiff of Maw's cooking and dismissed them for lunch. She hurried into the cafeteria, eager to approach Maw about spending Friday night with the Davis girls.

Maw didn't entirely approve of the girls, although she couldn't name any particular reason. Ginny Ruth figured that, because their giddiness seemed unnatural to Maw, she suspected they must be up to something.

Maw gave a reluctant yes, though she added a snort
36 of disapproval. Now Ginny Ruth could look forward

to her visit with the Davis sisters, as well as to hearing from the newspaper editor.

Ginny Ruth found an excuse to go into town every day after school. She wanted to check the post office box, which usually remained empty, except for an occasional advertisement about a bargain they couldn't afford to miss, according to Sears or Montgomery Ward. She wanted to be the one to find the newspaper in the box, should she be so fortunate as to have her poem accepted for publication.

It was Thursday when she peeked through the little glass door of the post office box and saw something crammed inside. Eagerly she called to Mr. Drummond to hand her the newspaper and envelope that were inside their box.

Mr. Billy, whom Ginny Ruth hadn't seen since Christmas Eve, shuffled into the post office while Mr. Drummond was retrieving her mail.

"Hi do, Mr. Billy!" Ginny Ruth called to him. "Mr. Drummond is fetching my mail! It's a newspaper and an envelope, Mr. Billy. Do you reckon they actually printed a poem of mine?"

Mr. Drummond returned. "My goodness, Ginny Ruth, this here paper is addressed to you personal!"

He came from behind the counter to stand next to Mr. Billy as they waited for Ginny Ruth to show them her treasure. The envelope was addressed to her, too. She opened it first. There were two quarters inside folded cardboard. The note with them thanked her for 37 her contribution and informed her that her copy of the newspaper would arrive under separate cover.

Ginny Ruth held up the money and note for Mr. Billy and Mr. Drummond to see.

"Well, Ginny Ruth?" Mr. Drummond said. "Let's see! I never knowed anybody that got their own words in a newspaper before. I want to see this for myself. Don't keep Billy and me awaitin'."

She looked at Mr. Billy. Although he couldn't force his face muscles into a smile, his eyes smiled at her. She felt encouraged to look.

Ginny Ruth slipped the brown wrapper band off the newspaper, being extra careful not to tear it. She wanted to prove that it had been addressed to her. Quickly she unfolded the paper and scanned the front page.

"There!" she said, pointing. "See? In the lower left-hand corner where it says Reader Contributions."

The two men moved in closer to read over her shoulder with her:

BLUEBONNETS
By Miss Ginny Ruth Grover (age 12) of Clemmons

> *Hundreds of tiny blue-capped heads*
> *Nodding in the breeze*
> *Little elfin ladies*
> *Taking your ease.*
> *But there's hoeing and canning*

And so much work to do,
Watch out you aren't crushed
Beneath some farmer's shoe.

"That's cute, Ginny Ruth!" Mr. Drummond said, patting her shoulder. "That's real cute. I'll declare, it is."

Above the poem, in darker print, it said, "A humorous poem."

Ginny Ruth couldn't look at Mr. Drummond or Mr. Billy. Her eyes stung with tears. And her chest ached from holding back the sobs that built there.

She had written that poem after the Reverend Trowbridge had told them in class about symbolism and how familiar things could be used to represent something else. She had intended the flowers to be like the women of Clemmons, who were eventually crushed like the bluebonnets beneath their farm burdens.

Tears spilled out and down her cheeks. Ginny Ruth crumpled the newspaper and threw it to the floor before running blindly through the door and into the road.

"It ain't cute," she whimpered. "And it ain't funny, neither."

FOUR

Ginny Ruth heaved with sobs as she ran toward home, oblivious to the frozen snow against her sandaled feet. By the time she reached their cabin, her eyes were puffy and dry and stung as if she'd caught a face full of nettles.

She'd planned to hurl the hateful notebook full of her secret thoughts into the fire, to be consumed just as her pride had been consumed at the post office. But her energy, like her emotions, was spent. She merely slunk to a corner of the cabin, whimpering like a kicked puppy.

When she remembered that Maw would be back soon from Mrs. Corbett's, where she'd gone to help with supper, Ginny Ruth washed her face. She wanted to hide her outburst as best she could.

Unable to avoid sulking, though, she mumbled an excuse to Maw. And she squeezed her eyes shut tightly, trying to conjure up the memory of Paw stroking her hair, murmuring, "It's okay, sweet patootie. It's gonna be okay, little darling."

Ginny Ruth didn't go back to the post office. She

didn't want to see Mr. Drummond, and she especially didn't want to see Mr. Billy right then. Oh, why had he tempted her into sharing her poem with that newspaper? How foolish she had looked!

The way her thoughts had been treated by that newspaper fellow gnawed at her the rest of the week. She tried reading the book of poetry that Miss Marnie had sent to her, but her heart wasn't in it. Besides, just as she'd gotten comfortable with rhyming poetry, this poet came along with poems that didn't rhyme at all. It was too puzzling to sort out in her current state of mind.

At school the chalk dust irritated her nose, and the scuffling feet offended her ears. Ginny Ruth took her anger out on her notepaper, so that her pencil point continually snapped and she ground it shorter and shorter at the wall sharpener.

On Friday she marched to the sharpener for what must have been the tenth time, choosing to ignore the reverend's suspicious glare. As she cranked the sharpener, she harbored visions of revenge. How would that editor like the door to his outhouse—if editors had such things—nailed shut? Ginny Ruth ambled back to her seat, grinning at the delicious thought.

She was suddenly aware of Lester Moore grinning back at her. He thought she was smiling at him! She tried scowling, but the damage was done. He looked like a Cheshire cat locked in a coop of chickens.

Ginny Ruth was grateful to be going home with the Davis sisters, to escape into their playful world that she so envied. When the alarm clock on the reverend's desk finally sounded and he dismissed them, she was the first one to reach the coat hooks at the back of the room.

Simultaneously Lester unfolded himself from his desk and was at her side. "It'd pleasure me to carry your books home, Ginny Ruth," he said.

She flushed, aware that Cyrilla and Daniel were observing the whole thing, crossing their eyes at her behind his back. She pretended ignorance. "Why, Lester, why ever would you want to take my books home with you?"

He shuffled his feet uncomfortably. "Naw, I mean, aw, Ginny Ruth, doggone it, you know what I mean, don't you?" Lester looked as if he were about to come apart.

"You know my maw don't cotton to me paying attention to boys," Ginny Ruth said. To tell the truth, she didn't really know what Maw thought about boys and her. But she could well imagine, and it did seem like an easy way to get away from Lester. She felt a mite sorry for him at that moment—he was easier to feel sorry for when the asafetida bag was downwind. "But, thank you anyway, Lester. That was right thoughtful of you to offer."

Lester seemed to recover quickly enough, racing out the door to catch up with the Randall boys. Ginny Ruth breathed a sigh of gratitude and joined the Davis girls on the short trip home. She did her best to endure their teasing about the incident good-naturedly.

The Davis house sprawled in every direction. Its rooms extended spiderlike from the original smaller structure to accommodate the large brood of girls who had been born into the family.

At the gate Ginny Ruth grinned and bent to scoop Francie into her arms, giving the warm, round child a big hug. Francie was yard age; she would start school next September, along with Elvira.

Grace, her legs as spindly and unsteady as a yearling's, toddled to claim her share of Ginny Ruth's attention. She was a porch child, not yet turned loose in the yard, where there was always the danger of an unwary child tangling with an irate rooster or wandering beneath the hooves of a grazing cow.

Hester was still pretty much a lap baby. And Mrs. Davis, much older in looks than in calendar years, was expecting another child in the spring.

The Davises named their children alphabetically. While Mr. Davis insisted that this new baby would be the long-awaited Isaac, Mrs. Davis was already resigned to carrying Imogene.

Rural life was especially hard on young children, and the infant mortality rate was high. The nearest doctor was in Stallings; a real hospital was thirty miles away. Some of the folks still had three or four children apiece, but many lost at least one to unattended illnesses or one of the multitude of indescribable farm accidents that occurred.

The Davis girls, however, somehow survived, even managed to thrive, so that their house grew and expanded almost biennially. Mrs. Davis not only remained good-humored through it all, but also managed to spread her love generously among the girls. She even had enough left over to lavish on Ginny Ruth when she visited.

Ginny Ruth planted a big, noisy kiss on the squirming, giggling Francie and hugged the gurgling Grace. Then she herself was swept into Mrs. Davis's arms in a warm and friendly greeting.

Mrs. Davis was a small woman, not even five feet tall, and Ginny Ruth was already overtaking her in size, just as three of her daughters had. The woman applied a friendly whack to Ginny Ruth's backside and said, "Apple turnovers in the keeper, girls. Then to your chores."

Mr. Davis worked at a repair shop for farm implements in Stallings. It wasn't much of a job, considering the poor farming in the area, but it enabled the Davises to buy laying hens and two milk cows so they had their own eggs and milk. They also had a good vegetable garden in season. Of course, it took a fair amount to feed a family of ten, going on eleven.

Visitors were expected to take part in the chores right along with the family. Although Ginny Ruth hated everything to do with farming, she found the work almost fun when it was shared with that happy brood.

44   It was tempting to help whoever drew the easier chores,

but Ginny Ruth generally went along with Cyrilla.

The chores were posted on a large piece of paper tacked to the kitchen door. The girls gathered around the list, moaning or snickering, depending on the chore assigned to them.

Cyrilla grabbed the wicker basket from the counter. "My turn to gather eggs. Come on with me, please," she coaxed.

Ginny Ruth wrinkled her nose. If there was one chore she really hated, it was gathering eggs. She hated it even more than cleaning out the cow stalls. She and chickens just didn't get along all that well.

"We have one old hen that's mighty protective of her eggs right now," Cyrilla warned her. "She won't give them up without a fight."

"I'm not afraid of something as little as a silly old setting hen," Ginny Ruth lied. She stepped into the dark hen house, nearly bolting when she caught the first whiff of its stench.

"Watch out for Big Red," Cyrilla warned. "I'm sure she's back there in the dark somewhere."

A few Plymouth Rocks and Bantams still sat in the waist-high nesting boxes filled with straw. They skittered through the door when the girls stepped inside, clucking at the interruption of the day's work. Ginny Ruth could see the gleaming white eggs and a few dark brown ones in the straw. She grabbed them and set them in the basket Cyrilla carried, anxious to leave as quickly as possible.

As she moved toward the back of the chicken house, she heard a low, guttural warning.

"She's back there," Cyrilla whispered. "Can you spot her?"

Ginny Ruth squinted in the dark, trying to make out any movement. Then she saw a tiny glint of light reflected in the eyes of the hen. Her dark form hovered menacingly over her cache of eggs.

Ginny Ruth reached into the dark, but retracted her hand, screaming in pain as she felt a quick, sharp peck. The Rhode Island Red gave another guttural warning.

She hated to let the hen get the best of her, especially in front of Cyrilla, who seemed to fear nothing in this world or the next. Ginny Ruth waved her right hand overhead, trying to attract the hen's attention, but the hen went unerringly for the left hand that had reached out for the egg.

Suddenly, with a flapping of wings and an angry squawk, Big Red flew at her head. Razor-sharp claws caught in Ginny Ruth's hair. Screaming like a wounded coyote, Ginny Ruth ran into the yard, the hen still attached to her hair.

The panicked hen flapped one more time against her, then settled onto the fence post when Ginny Ruth finally came to a dead stop at the well. The hen continued to squawk angrily at Ginny Ruth, who sank to the ground, panting hard.

46   Cyrilla ran to her and leaned over, a look of fear

etched across her face. "Are you all right? Speak to me!"

Ginny Ruth shook her head. "Whew, I feel like I got caught in a dust devil! Am I bleeding?"

Cyrilla inspected Ginny Ruth's scalp. "No punctures, but you do look like you might have been tangling with a bull instead of a little bitty old setting hen!" She patted Ginny Ruth's hair back into place.

"Little bitty old hen, nothing!" Ginny Ruth snorted. "She's the devil's daughter! Eggs or no eggs, I'm not going back in that hen house!"

With a final warning, the hen strutted back to the hen house and resumed her position in the nesting box.

Cyrilla sniggered. "You don't have to go back. I managed to get the eggs while you were keeping Big Red entertained."

Ginny Ruth laughed. "I'll expect a coddled egg in the morning for that, Miss Cyrilla!"

"Let's get these inside before they get broken," Cyrilla said. "I still have to tote a couple of jars of corn and peas out of the storm cellar for supper tonight."

When they'd put the eggs in the kitchen, Cyrilla lit an oil lantern. "Papa never did find a flashlight he thought was worth a durn," she said, blowing out the match.

They scrambled across the yard toward the mound of earth that was the storm cellar. Like most in that 47 area, it had been carved out of the ground and was a safe shelter during the twisters—cyclones or tornadoes—that harassed the area. But at other times it offered cool, dark storage for the vegetables and meats that were canned during season.

The girls had almost reached the wooden door that covered the entrance when Ginny Ruth suddenly gasped. "Oh, my gosh! Cyrilla, look!"

Smoke wisped, then puffed through the cracks of the door that was almost flat against the mound of dirt, which was the cellar's roof.

"Fire!" Cyrilla screeched. "Help me, Ginny Ruth! Get the bucket!"

The girls ran to the well and quickly dropped the attached wooden bucket down the length of the rope until they heard it splash. They felt it grow heavy with water.

"Oh, hurry!" Cyrilla begged, jerking at the rope. The metal pulley made a steady, raucous creak as the two of them yanked frantically at the rope. At last they had the bucket back on the edge of the brick wall surrounding the well. Cyrilla unhooked the bucket, and the girls, carrying the heavy, sloshing bucket between them, half stumbled, half ran toward the cellar.

"When I count to three, we'll heave the water," Cyrilla instructed as they struggled to the cellar door.

"One, two, *three!*"

They flung the bucket so that the water dropped in

one big splash onto the smoke that billowed through the crack in the door.

A shriek pierced the air. Then Beta, a corn-silk cigarette still clutched between her fingers, emerged, coughing and sputtering, from the cellar. The water had caught her broadside, and her hair and dress clung limply to her. She was still shrieking and coughing.

Ginny Ruth burst into giggles. "Beta! You were smoking?"

Cyrilla dropped the empty bucket and held her sides as she flopped onto the still-frozen ground in gales of laughter.

Beta flung down the cigarette and stepped on it, finally giving in to the giggles herself. "I wasn't having very good luck with it anyway," she said. "I don't know what they see in it, myself."

The girls got the vegetables from the cellar, then helped Beta dry off. The three of them were given to fits of giggles during supper that evening, although they continued to decline explanation as to what could be all that funny.

When supper was over, the girls scooted Mr. and Mrs. Davis off to sit in the parlor. Then they rallied around the sink in the kitchen. Within the hour they had the dishes washed, dried, and put away.

Daniel and Cyrilla put the smaller children to bed. Then the rest of them gathered by the parlor fireplace for some hot camomile tea and tea cookies, Ginny Ruth's favorite.

The small radio had broken, and Mr. Davis made excuses not to have it fixed in Stallings. "What with the terrible news and the worse music, the radio is better off broken. If you get to missing music too much, I'll get out my guitar," he teased. But since there were no takers, he retrieved his poultry journal from the side table and excused himself.

"Oh, I almost forgot, Alpha," Mrs. Davis said. Her eyes danced mischievously. "A letter came for you today. It's on the end table next to the Bible."

Alpha all but knocked over her teacup getting to the table. The other Davis girls whispered and giggled among themselves as Cyrilla winked at Ginny Ruth to signal that one of their infamous Davis tricks was about to begin.

Ginny Ruth wiggled in anticipation. She never knew what they would be up to next, but she could always count on its being fun.

Daniel assumed an air of the mysterious as she leaned over the teacup that Alpha had abandoned on the hearth. "Ah! I see it in the leaves; you have a letter from a loved one."

Alpha's mouth slacked slightly, but she quickly recovered her composure and shot a chilling glance at her sister. "You're just guessing! Or you've probably read the return address." She clutched the letter to her breast protectively and retreated to the light of the table lamp.

50   "Oh, unbeliever!" Daniel chanted. The other girls

snickered. Ginny Ruth set down her own cup to observe more closely.

"I will tell you the contents of the letter. I will read it in the leaves of your cup," Daniel sang. She turned the cup upside down on its saucer.

Alpha shrugged. "That's impossible, and you know it. I haven't even opened it yet."

"The tea leaves know all and tell all," Daniel chanted. "It is written in the leaves that your loved one is coming to see you soon. Very soon he will be here." She paused, turning the saucer slightly and frowning at it. "In ten days," she continued. "He will be wearing a soldier's uniform. But he will have another stripe on this uniform. Yes, I see it now. He is a corporal."

Alpha ripped open the letter and leaned toward the lamp, her mouth opening wider as she read. She turned to stare at Daniel. "Why, everything you said, it's true! James is coming home. And he—"

She stared at the saucer, then at Daniel. "You really see all that in there?"

Daniel held the cup above her head dramatically. "The tea leaves know all and tell all to the gifted eye. I am getting more vibrations now. James calls you his—"

Alpha snatched the cup and saucer from Daniel. "Never mind what he calls me! Stop this!" She ran from the room as the sisters burst into laughter.

Mrs. Davis grinned, shaking her head. "Girls, girls, what am I going to do with you? Teasing a poor lovestruck girl like that! Off to bed with the lot of you now!" 51

Ginny Ruth hugged Mrs. Davis good night. The girls lit the kerosene lantern, and the three of them traipsed to the outhouse. The Davises had a room set aside for a real bathroom someday, but, like most Clemmons folks, they had to postpone that luxury. As much as Ginny Ruth dreaded the outhouse at night, she hated the thought of the indoor chamber pot more.

Back inside, Ginny Ruth slipped into her granny gown, which she saved for such special occasions as this. Maw had made it from one of the old shirts Paw had left behind, and Ginny Ruth felt snug just knowing it had once been his.

Alpha and Beta had their own bedroom. Cyrilla and Daniel ordinarily shared the small bedroom with Elvira, but she had been shifted for the night to Francie and Grace's room.

Daniel slipped into the narrow bed and yawned broadly. She was asleep almost instantly. The moon had come out and streamed through the thin, cotton curtains at the window, slashing the dark room in half.

Ginny Ruth and Cyrilla slid beneath the thick goose-down comforter on the double bed, whispering so as not to wake Daniel. Ginny Ruth pulled the comforter up to her chin and felt its caressing comfort even before the toasty warmth set in. "What Daniel did tonight was wonderful," Ginny Ruth said. "I had no idea she was so gifted."

Cyrilla tittered. "She isn't, silly! Daniel steamed that 52 letter open this afternoon and read it. Then she resealed it. Daniel does that all the time, and love-sick old Alpha never seems to catch on to it."

"Oh," Ginny Ruth whispered, disappointed. "I see." She couldn't share her friend's mirth.

"I thought you'd think that was funny, Ginny Ruth," Cyrilla scolded. "What's the matter with you anyway?"

Ginny Ruth slid farther under the goose-down comforter. "Nothing, I suppose," she said, sighing heavily. "I guess it's just that I was hoping Daniel could see into the future for real. I'd like a bit of a hint of my own."

Cyrilla assumed the same chanting voice that Daniel had used earlier. "The tea leaves know all and tell all. Ginny Ruth Grover will marry Lester Moore and have many more Moores."

Ginny Ruth sat bolt upright, slamming the comforter down to her knees. "Don't ever say that again, Cyrilla!"

Daniel gave a muffled protest and Ginny Ruth lowered her voice. "I'll never marry a Clemmons boy! I'd sooner die!"

"It's cold!" Cyrilla protested, pulling the cover back up. "Alpha's beau is a Clemmons boy. When he gets out of the army I expect they'll get married." She yawned, then added huffily, "At least Clemmons boys stay put."

Ginny Ruth felt her ears burn with anger. She knew that last remark was aimed at her "ne'er-do-well" paw. She lay down and rolled over with her back to Cyrilla, 53 pretending to sleep so she wouldn't have to talk any more.

She listened to the tin roof above them contracting and settling in the cold night air. Words, thoughts floated to her consciousness. She squeezed her eyes shut and clamped her hands over her ears to shut them out. She didn't want the poems to come. She hated being laughed at by strangers, even by those she called friends. But the words came anyway, teasing her, challenging her to embrace them.

> When my heart is aching,
> A true friend cares.
> The burden's not so heavy when
> A true friend shares.
> Oh, where is my true friend
> who cares and shares?

FIVE

Outside the bedroom window, a rooster crowed stridently. Ginny Ruth stretched and blinked at her surroundings, for a moment not remembering where she was. Cyrilla was gone. Good enough, she thought; she wouldn't have to face her just yet.

She rolled over to look out the window. A gray dawn was peeking through the frosted window. Fog still swirled and hovered outside.

Ginny Ruth pushed away the soft, warm comforter slightly, allowing the cool air to rush against her face. Except in the kitchen, where the cooking stove would be fired up by now, and the living room, there was no heat in the house, and what little warmth had been stored up from the day before had long since dissipated.

The rooster crowed again. Ginny Ruth gave a resigned sigh, then threw back the covers and swung her bare feet to the floor. The icy wood sent a chill racing through her body, and her feet slapped against it as she hopped from one foot to the other, quickly slipping into her sandals, which were, alas, no warmer.

Ginny Ruth dressed quickly, then snatched her coat 55

and slipped down the path toward the outhouse. She ran smack into Cyrilla, who was on her way back to the house.

"Mornin'!" Cyrilla greeted her, as if her last words to Ginny Ruth hadn't been the most hateful ever.

Determined to be civil—after all, she was a guest—Ginny Ruth nodded, although she could feel her jaw tense. She was aware of a vein pulsing at her temple. "Mornin'." She jammed her hands into her pockets and trotted on to the outhouse.

As she wove her way through the begging chickens back to the house, she made up her mind. Maybe her own words to Cyrilla had been a mite unkind—after all, Cyrilla's papa was a Clemmons man. And the Davis girls—if they married at all—would probably wind up with Clemmons men. She would be polite. She had half a day to spend there or a lot of explaining to do to Maw. She would pretend that last night hadn't happened.

Sharing, caring, the quiet voice inside her said. Wasn't that supposed to go both ways? Ginny Ruth had seen a look of anxiety about Cyrilla's eyes; she was probably sorry for her hurtful words.

The unmistakable smell of bacon and eggs mingled with the smell of fresh biscuits reached her as she let herself in through the unpainted back door. One thing about the Davises, Ginny Ruth admitted, they ate well, probably better than anyone in Clemmons. Somehow their vegetable garden flourished, their cow never dried up, and their chickens multiplied and layed with regularity. Their few acres of land seemed truly blessed.

Ginny Ruth helped the girls set the table with fresh-churned butter and syrup for the biscuits. Then, gratefully, she dug into the platter of eggs and bacon as it was passed.

It was Saturday, but that didn't mean a day off in rural Texas. Life went on. Cows still needed milking, eggs needed gathering, and any other chores that were left over from the week needed to be done.

Usually that meant washing and bluing the week's worth of laundry in a large cauldron that sat outside over a low fire. There was a washeteria in Stallings, but it seemed a sin to cart all the dirty laundry twelve miles down the road and to stand in line when a cauldron had been good enough for the forebears. And the money spent on the trip was better spent for food.

The Drummonds, who had installed indoor water and a butane water heater, had gone so far as to get a washing machine back when the Clemmons economy was better. But the machine had broken down, and repairmen didn't live down the corner. Now it sat on the front porch, a couple of pot plants gracing its top.

Clemmons was an odd mixture of early pioneer America and the few modern conveniences it had taken to its bosom. Although houses were lighted with electricity—those that hadn't lost it for nonpayment—most 57 were heated by wood. Most folks, like Ginny Ruth's maw, still cooked with wood, although a few had butane cooking stoves.

Some folks had their wells attached to pump water right into their kitchens, but only a few houses had actually gone so modern as to have indoor bathrooms. Maw thought it was downright unsanitary, in fact. Bathing was done with water heated from a stove and poured into a large metal tub brought out for the occasion.

Money was the main problem. There wasn't any. But Ginny Ruth remembered a few years ago when a government fella had visited Clemmons. He had told them about some kind of aid they could get and brought a passel of papers for them to fill out. He had wanted answers to too many personal questions, though, and the folks had all but run him out of town.

On second thought, Ginny Ruth figured it must be pride, not money or the lack of it, that was the main problem in Clemmons. When a town was as isolated as Clemmons, it just naturally clung to what it did have and became all the more resistant to change. Its family feuds, like the one between Maw and her folks, were till death. And its feelings toward outsiders were hostile.

While the Davis girls finished their chores, Ginny Ruth gathered the young children in the warmer part of the house. She got the Montgomery Ward and Sears catalogs down from the shelf and helped them to cut out the ladies for paper dolls. They made flour paste and pasted pictures of curtains and furniture from the catalogs to shoe boxes for their dollhouses.

When Grace tore the head from her doll, Ginny Ruth glued it together for her. Francie, meanwhile, had her two dolls deep in conversation and action.

Ginny Ruth held her own cutout dolls, but she found herself more content to watch Francie and Grace playing out their drama. She frowned, remembering what fun it had been, she and Cyrilla imagining themselves to be those ladies, living in their pretty houses. But things had begun to change. First there were her gradually swelling breasts, then the periods. Maw had sat her down and told her gravely that she was a woman now, and she had the responsibility to be a good one. Of course, she turned right around and said Ginny Ruth was too young to go into Stallings to the picture show. So much for womanhood!

Ginny Ruth had learned a lot from the two Davis girls ahead of her and from the magazines they sneak-read. The Davises thought growing up was going to be wonderful. Maw seemed to think it was a tragedy. Ginny Ruth figured it was just a big bother, although she was trying to withhold judgment for the moment. She had begun to see it as her first step toward getting out of Clemmons, and that made it a lot more welcome.

Handing her own dolls to Grace, Ginny Ruth heaved a sigh; she reckoned she had turned another 59 corner. It was as if there were a great big hole in her and she didn't have anything to fill the hole with yet. It was such a different kind of emptiness from the one she felt because of Paw.

After a lunch of soup and leftover biscuits, Ginny Ruth hugged Mrs. Davis good-bye and swallowed her pride enough to thank Cyrilla for a good time. She left with her feelings for Cyrilla all mixed up.

At home she greeted Maw, who was on her way to sit with the still-sick Mrs. Corbett. Ginny Ruth paced back and forth, trying to fight off the words that formed in her mind. She didn't want to write any more. It hurt too much when people laughed. But the words pressed at her until finally she snatched the notebook from beneath her mattress and let her pencil hover over the fresh page. She sighed. "I guess I can't *not* write."

> *Half woman and*
> *Half girl*
> *Caught suspended,*
> *Caught in a whirl*
> *Too old for paper dolls*
> *But too young to leave,*
> *Too sad to laugh*
> *Too glad to grieve.*

She cocked her head to one side, tapping her lip with the pencil. Would that make sense to anyone but 60   her? she wondered. She slammed the notebook shut and jammed it under her mattress. What did she care if anyone else could make sense of it? She was never going to share her thoughts again.

The next day was Sunday. Being the only day that the hard-working folks of Clemmons actually felt compelled to do no work, it was quite social. Ginny Ruth scrubbed extra hard, although Maw couldn't show her any place in the Bible where it said that cleanliness was next to godliness. Then the two of them walked the well-traveled path to the small frame building that was the Baptist church.

The Reverend Trowbridge, her teacher all week long and now her pastor, stood in the chilly foyer, greeting his spiritual flock. Widowed only last year, he was the object of warm smiles from the unattached ladies of Baptist persuasion, although none of them dared make their moves until the usual mourning period—six months maximum—was complete.

The Methodist church, just over the hill, had no resident minister. Instead it had a circuit preacher who arrived every third Sunday from Stallings. He was young, with a dark handlebar moustache, and church attendance was always up on his Sundays. The front pews were filled with all the eligible young Methodist women, who prayed that he'd notice them.

The few families who were of other denominations generally piled into the pickup truck with the most gas, or the least-bald tires, and rode up to Stallings. One way or the other, most houses in Clemmons emptied   61 out on Sunday, since the town was unified in its God-fearing ways.

Clemmons was in a dry county, which meant no liquor could be sold, bought, or consumed there. That was the legal definition. What it really meant was that traffic was heavy on the farm road into the next county, where some of the good folks of Clemmons, who voted for dry and shouted their amens on Sunday mornings, did their drinking.

The exception was Piney Jenkins. He could usually be seen sleeping one off in a doorway, unless by some miracle he managed to make it all the way home two hills away.

The pious ladies would cluck and fuss and cross the street to keep their precious children from seeing such a disgusting sight. It was likely, though, that Piney had paid more than one of those young innocents to fetch him a bottle from his still, which was hidden about a half mile inside the woods.

Ginny Ruth felt particularly pensive that morning. She sat absently through the Sunday-school lesson being taught by Miss Nettie Pritchert, who still referred to herself as "one of the girls," although Paw had called her "over the hill" three years ago.

She leaned her chair back on two legs until it nearly slid out from under her, and she picked at a small ravel in her dress until it became a large ravel. Still Miss Pritchert just kept on cawing about the evils of one thing or another, until religion sounded like no fun at all.

Ginny Ruth sighed with relief when the bell rang at last, calling an end to the lesson so that church could begin. Not that she was all that eager for church, but it meant only one hour more before she could go home. Unless, she reminded herself, the reverend was feeling particularly called upon to end sin in Clemmons once and for all. Then it might be an hour and a half.

Miss Nettie dipped her head, murmured a quick dismissal prayer, then scooted off to the sanctuary where she started her second and most important function in the church—playing the pump organ. Lester, not good for much else that Ginny Ruth could determine, except embarrassing her to the blushes, did the pumping while Miss Nettie ran her nimble fingers over the keys, nodding her head in time.

If Lester pumped hard and kept pumping steadily, the organ sounded fair. But if he stopped to rest, the music went flat and sounded more like a discontented bull than like heavenly notes.

Ginny Ruth joined Maw in the third pew right, next to the Drummonds, who nodded a greeting. The pews were varnished to look like mahogany, but no one was fooled in the least.

There were two potbelly stoves, one at the front of the church and one at the back, in the center aisle.

The reverend used to light both of them, until he discovered that folks left the front pews empty. Once he used only the front stove, the congregation flooded the front pews, more to his satisfaction.

Ginny Ruth scooted over, trying to look like two people so folks wouldn't be reminded of Paw's continued absence. There were no cushions, and sometimes it felt to Ginny Ruth that she was being pushed right through until she became a part of the wood. In the winter the wood was cold against her legs, and in the summer she became glued to the bare wood by her own sweat. She ran her fingers over the cold wood, feeling the indentations where several generations of disobedient children had carved their names.

Ginny Ruth glanced to the left and front, where she spotted the Simmses in their regular pew, looking content with themselves. Nobody really owned a pew, but it seemed that they all had staked their claims on certain ones long ago, and they never moved.

Ginny Ruth was tempted to be sitting in the Simmses' spot some Sunday morning when they got there, just to see what they'd do. Would they take someone else's place and start a whole reshuffling of bodies? Or had she become so invisible to them that they'd just sit right down on her?

She wondered if they ever tried to snatch quick glances at her, looking for a familiar dimple or a certain hue to the eye. Well, let them, she thought with some satisfaction. They'd find nothing of themselves except maybe the caramel color of her hair. She took after Paw strictly, and that suited her just fine.

Miss Nettie played "Onward, Christian Soldiers" to drown out the shuffling feet as the folks made their way down the aisle and to their seats. Then the organ sounded a loud, slightly off-key chord, which Miss Nettie no doubt blamed on Lester, and the whole congregation rose and mumbled "Blessed Be the Tie That Binds," which always initiated the service.

The Reverend Trowbridge made his entrance then, ending up at the pulpit when the congregation sang "Amen," even though Miss Nettie had to drag out the last note to make the timing right. She'd seen it done that way in Stallings once and was bound and determined to do it herself.

Ginny Ruth shifted from one foot to the other while the preacher led them in a lengthy prayer for everything from an early spring and good planting to the souls of the sinners who consorted with the devil on Saturday night. She took it he meant poor old Piney, who was lying in the bank doorway that very morning.

She kept the eye nearest Maw closed but squinted the other one so she could see Cyrilla, who never stopped chattering during the prayer. There was a shuffling of feet and coughing and throat clearing as the Reverend Trowbridge completed his prayer. Then he made his announcements. "There will be a prayer meeting on Wednesday, which will be followed by an ice-cream social," he said.

65

Ginny Ruth licked her lips at the thought. She didn't find joy in going out in the cold night to do more singing and praying, but the ice cream sounded inviting. Even in the dead of winter, it would guarantee high attendance for the prayer meeting.

"Mrs. Rogers will have a quilting party on Friday morning. You ladies rummage through your rag bags and participate in this fine activity," the Reverend Trowbridge said. He cleared his throat. "And now the deacons will pass the offering plate among you. Remember the story of the widow's mites and do likewise."

Lester jumped up to the organ to pump again, and Miss Nettie began a lively rendition of "Bringing in the Sheaves." She played it well because she never varied in her choices of music, and practice does make perfect, folks say.

Ginny Ruth twitched, waiting for the plate to pass her. She liked to touch its cold surface as it made its way swiftly through the congregation with an occasional clinking sound.

Guiltily she remembered the shiny fifty cents still tucked inside her notebook, the money the newspaper editor had paid her for her "humorous poem." If she were a proper tither, as the reverend wanted them to be, she'd be dropping in a nickel of that right now. She told herself that the Lord probably didn't want hateful money, and that was what it was. Besides, if the Lord wanted everybody to give him ten percent of everything, why didn't he take away ten percent of the hurt and pain? It seemed only fair.

The reverend prayed again, this time for the Lord to give him the right words, and there was a general clearing of throats and coughing again as the folks settled in for his sermon.

He moved into it with vigor, pounding the pulpit with his fist. "I entreat you, good people, to remove the malice from your hearts. Make room for love! Sweet Christian love! Where there is malice there is no room for kind thoughts." He raised his outstretched hands to heaven. "O Lord, gentle their hearts!"

Ginny Ruth shifted uncomfortably. She had to agree, she had just about all the malice that could be held in one heart, but if she got rid of that, who was to say there wouldn't be a plain old empty hole there?

The preacher was perspiring now, although the stove was burning low. He dipped his head, praying that a lost one would come forward during the music that would be playing soon.

Lester jumped up and pumped, and Miss Nettie started playing "Just As I Am." She played the second, third, and fourth verses, and the congregation sang. But no one moved forward.

"You're out there!" the Reverend Trowbridge shouted above the music. He mopped sweat from his brow with a crumpled white handkerchief. "Lost souls, I know you're there. And God knows you're there."

Ginny Ruth twisted in her seat to look around. She

saw the Gaithers, who seemed to be having their hell on earth, so what more could God want from them? And there was dear, sweet Miss Marnie, whose biggest sin was an overdue library book; the Simmses, who must already have considered themselves perfect, since they saw fit to pass judgment on their descendants; Mr. Randall, who didn't even slip off to Stallings to "wet his whistle"; and the Moores, who had Lester for a son, and wasn't that enough penance? It was the same crowd of folks that had been there every Sunday for as long as she could remember.

People who didn't meet their moral standards got promptly churched, which ought to be called un-churched, because that was exactly what happened. They were thrown out of the "fellowship." That didn't exactly make for a large crowd of lost souls for the good reverend to call to his bosom.

The congregation ran out of verses to sing, but Miss Nettie kept playing softer, and the people hummed to the music. The preacher had given a whopping good sermon, Ginny Ruth figured, and if there were any lost souls they would surely have come forward by now.

Ginny Ruth's stomach growled. There were rumbles from stomachs all over the church. Mr. Randall had stopped looking at his watch and was thumping and shaking it vigorously.

The Reverend Trowbridge sighed heavily, dropping
his hands to his sides in surrender. There were no souls

for saving that Sunday. He raised his hands palms down over the congregation and squeezed his eyes shut. "Lord, Lord," he moaned, slowly working his way down the aisle, "you know their hearts better than I."

Ginny Ruth saw him pass their pew, heading for the front door. Nobody was going to get out without coming face to face with him.

"Touch them this week, O Lord. Touch them and bring them to Thy holy ways. Amen."

The congregation stood anchored to their pews, their eyes closed, until Miss Nettie broke into the tune of "Onward, Christian Soldiers" once more.

When Miss Nettie hit the last note, Lester stood up, panting hard. He winked at Ginny Ruth behind her maw's back. Ginny Ruth returned his look with a narrow glare, then followed Maw into the yard, which was a bit warmer now that the sun was finally straight up. Folks were lingering there to share a week's worth of gossip and rheumatism complaints.

Maw nodded to Mrs. Rachel Rogers, then went over to explain that she couldn't be at the quilting, since she'd be cooking at the school on Friday. It was something Mrs. Rogers already knew, of course, but Maw was bent on doing what seemed right to her.

Ginny Ruth kicked loose a stone that was embedded in the ground, trying to keep herself entertained while Maw talked. Out of the corner of her eye she saw Mrs. Gaither motioning to her.

69

She hesitated, remembering that she hadn't seen Mr. Billy since she'd run from the post office in a huff over the poem. She didn't particularly want to see him just yet, but Mrs. Gaither motioned again. Then the vision of the Christmas treats brushed away her reluctance, and she moved through the crowd to stand in front of them, staring shyly at her feet, which protruded grotesquely from her sandals.

Mr. Billy muttered something to her, and hesitantly Ginny Ruth cocked her head to squint in his direction. She realized her mouth was shut as tight as Maw's and forced it into a grin.

"He wants to give you something," Mrs. Gaither interpreted. Ginny Ruth figured it took a lot of practice to understand Mr. Billy.

Mr. Billy poked toward Ginny Ruth something that was wrapped in a piece of tissue.

"For me?" Ginny Ruth asked. "Why, it ain't my birthday or nothing!"

Mrs. Gaither nodded toward the package. "Open it, child. It won't bite. And it is something of a special occasion."

Curiously Ginny Ruth pulled the tissue back, revealing a small pewter picture frame. Under the glass was the clipping of her poem, but the hateful words "humorous poem" had been cut away.

She swallowed hard, staring at the framed poem, 70 then raised her eyes to look into Mr. Billy's liquid blue ones. She reached out swiftly to squeeze his trembling hand, to hold it steady for just a moment.

Then she turned away and ran to join Maw. She couldn't say anything—not just then.

SIX

Ginny Ruth tucked the frame inside her pocket as Miss Marnie, dressed in her fur-trimmed coat, approached her. "Hi do, Ginny Ruth," she greeted, taking her hand.

"Hi do, Miss Marnie," Ginny Ruth returned. "I thank you for sending along that poetry book. I don't rightly understand why they are poems when they don't rhyme, but there are some right nice thoughts in there. I'll get it back to you soon."

"There is no hurry, Ginny Ruth. I purchased that book in Stallings years ago. I thought it might be time to introduce such an intelligent young lady as yourself to a greater variety, not that I don't thrill to Longfellow and the like, you understand."

"Yes'm. I reckon it is that I take comfort in knowing what might come next. When I know it's going to rhyme, it's a little like following a road map."

Miss Marnie glanced around, then leaned closer to whisper. "I declare, Ginny Ruth, you certainly surprised me the other day, getting your very own words

72

printed in a newspaper. I flush with pride, thinking that maybe—just maybe—I might have played a small part in that, introducing you to some of the finer writers and all. Now, don't tell me if I didn't because it will surely shatter all my grand illusions!"

Ginny Ruth dipped her head, flushing at the mention of the poem.

"It was quite sensitive, Ginny Ruth, and it was a fine use of . . . of metaphor."

"But the newspaper feller said it was humorous, Miss Marnie!" Ginny Ruth said. Her lip trembled as she remembered.

"And he is a stupid fellow. It wouldn't surprise me at all if he got an irate letter regarding that fact."

"You? You wrote a letter about my poem, Miss Marnie?"

Miss Marnie patted Ginny Ruth's arm reassuringly. "I'm sure I'm not the only intelligent reader, child. You just keep writing now, you hear? I expect some day to send off to Dallas for a book with your name on it, Ginny Ruth. And I'll tell them all that I know you."

Ginny Ruth tried to visualize that future scene, but nothing came. "Yes'm." She saw Cyrilla making gestures at her, and Maw was beginning to look a mite impatient, so she thanked Miss Marnie, excusing herself. It was one thing to have friends praise your words, as Miss Marnie did, and as Mr. Billy did by framing them. But strangers had to like them, too, didn't they?   73

Ginny Ruth stepped quickly toward Maw, but she was stopped by Cyrilla, who grabbed her arm. "Hidy," Cyrilla greeted. "Daniel and me are going to Trisa Corbett's this afternoon. You wanna come, too?"

Ginny Ruth pulled loose. "No, thank you. I have some important stuff to do this afternoon."

Cyrilla grabbed her arm again. "You got a burr under your blanket for something, Ginny Ruth Grover. What did I do to get you all het up at me?"

Squaring her shoulders, Ginny Ruth shook Cyrilla's grip loose. "If you really don't know, I didn't like what you said the other night. I know you meant my paw when you said Clemmons boys stay put!"

Cyrilla stiffened. "Well, you weren't all that kind to my paw, either. You act so high and mighty sometimes, as if you're better than the rest of us."

Ginny Ruth melted a little. "I don't mean that. It's just . . . just, I don't have the same . . . I want more than Clemmons can . . ." Why couldn't she find the words now to express the feelings she had? "Neither of us is wrong, Cyrilla. We're just different, that's all." She jammed her hands into her pockets, feeling the small frame there.

"I didn't intend to hurt your feelings, Ginny Ruth," Cyrilla said. Her voice sounded stiff, formal. "But your paw—"

Ginny Ruth's fingers wrapped around the frame. She jerked it from her pocket. "Was here Christmas," she interrupted. "I guess I just forgot to tell you. He came up that path on Christmas Eve, bringing me candy and oranges and this here picture frame with my poem in it. We had a wonderful visit. He played his guitar and we sang songs and . . ."

Maw always told her the angels wept when she told a lie. She didn't know if there were tears in heaven at that very moment, but her throat sure ached from the lump forming there. Those lies were nearly choking her.

Cyrilla's face mirrored the suspicion she most surely felt right then. "You'd think you'd mention an important thing like that to your best friend. So how come he didn't stay?"

"Why, he had to get back to work . . . in Dallas," Ginny Ruth said. It was too late to stop. "He's in Dallas, earning lots of money. When he has enough, me 'n' Maw are going to live with him."

Ginny Ruth held her breath. Good friends might not believe that pack of lies, but they would be willing to pretend. Was Cyrilla that good a friend?

Cyrilla gave Ginny Ruth a quick hug, although the flat expression in her eyes showed her doubt. "That would be wonderful." She dipped her head slightly in a quick farewell, then raced off to her family.

Ginny Ruth joined Maw, and the two of them walked home silently. Maw was deep in her own thoughts, and Ginny Ruth was busy wishing she could wipe out the last thirty minutes of her life.

At home she tucked away the framed poem, deciding 75

to pull it from her secret hiding place only on special occasions. As she thought more about it, she realized it wasn't impossible that Paw would see the poem. And if he did he would clip it and eventually send it to her, just as she'd said. She was almost beginning to believe it herself.

She pulled out the book Miss Marnie had lent her and read. Maw didn't scold her for her idleness. She figured that Ginny Ruth was honor bound to read something Miss Marnie had lent her. There were poems about a sunrise as seen from a tree, about an anthill, about the most ordinary of things. Yet each had a kind of beauty about it.

"Maw," Ginny Ruth asked. "Do you think there is any beauty in Clemmons?"

Maw put down her mending. "You know, your paw said if you travel far enough, down toward Houston, the land is as flat as a hotcake. And if you go west enough, you don't see no trees at all."

When Maw talked about Paw and they weren't arguing about him, there was a certain dancing to her eyes, a relaxing of her jaw that made her look downright pretty. It seldom happened, and Ginny Ruth liked it. "I expect it is a mite easier walking when you don't have hills to contend with," she said.

Maw's mouth twisted into an almost smile. "Easier, I reckon. But can you imagine how plain and boring it must look? Why, Paw said the ground ain't even red—said it was kinda dark gray, or brown maybe, said it was like no color at all."

"Do you really think this old red dust is pretty, Maw?" Ginny Ruth asked.

"I didn't think nothin' about it till your paw told me about that other. I . . . I reckon I prefer red to that."

"Would you live in a flat place, a place with ugly ground, Maw? I mean if Paw was to—"

Maw's face hardened again. "It ain't gonna happen, missy. So jest get that outta your head." She snatched up her mending, ending Ginny Ruth's heady speculation.

Over the next few weeks, Ginny Ruth tried to see Clemmons with fresh eyes. The sun was coming up earlier now; the ice was melting into a pink liquid. The water pump in the schoolyard had thawed and was dripping, forming a puddle of red around it.

The paths around the seesaw and swings were cut deeply into the ground, but bright green shoots of salt grass peeked through the red dirt. Soon the hard, dry summer would coat everything with the fine, red dust. Could it really be beautiful? she wondered. Might she find words that could make it so?

One Saturday Ginny Ruth looked at their cabin in its stand of second-growth pines and sparse grass. With the white blanket gone, it looked bare and lonely. She found the seeds she'd given Maw for Christmas; it was time to plant them. The days were growing longer and 77 warmer, and the seeds would begin to sprout soon.

With a tablespoon she dug into the ground, loosening it to receive the seeds. She planted them on each side of the door, just as they must have been planted to look like the pictures in the magazine.

Ginny Ruth walked down the road that led into town, noting that many families were already working in their fields, feverishly turning the ground in readiness for spring planting. A dog barked to her left. A cow, its bell clanging with each lumbering step, moved past her on its way to pasture, marking the path with dung. Could one of those poets find beauty in that? she wondered. Maybe it was easier to see the beauty of Clemmons if you knew you weren't bound to it by poverty, if you knew you could leave it.

Passing the Gaithers', Ginny Ruth spotted Mr. Billy in the yard. He was pulling weeds from the ground around a gnarled gray vine that spiraled about the front porch, embracing it.

She smiled, remembering his two kindnesses to her. She wished she could repay him without offending what Maw called his pride. But how? she wondered.

On impulse she pushed through the creaking front gate and was nearly knocked to the ground by Mr. Billy's coon dog, Scaredy Cat, who barked and jumped delightedly.

"Hi do," she greeted Mr. Billy as she stooped to scratch Scaredy Cat behind the ears.

Mr. Billy nodded to her and mumbled something.

She stood watching him snatch at the weeds, his hands shaking so badly at times that he was barely able to grab hold.

"Mr. Billy," Ginny Ruth said, an idea springing into her head, "I have one of the biggest favors in my whole life to ask you."

When he looked up at her she continued. "I've been thinking of hiring myself out for the summer to earn a little money. But I need some experience, I do. I'd appreciate it if you'd allow me to work a bit around here doing odd jobs—for free, of course, since I'm just learning—to get myself a little job experience."

Mr. Billy's expression was one of puzzlement. So Ginny Ruth assumed a look of absolute pleading—one she'd perfected on Paw—just to emphasize that he'd be doing *her* the favor. She felt pleased that she was saving his pride.

Ginny Ruth dropped to the ground before he could answer. "Let me start right here," she said. She pulled enthusiastically at the weeds.

"Are you sure this here thing ain't dead, Mr. Billy?" she asked. "It sure looks like it. I could dig it out if you have a shovel somewheres."

Mr. Billy mumbled something, but the expression in his eyes told her more. He pulled a bit of the vine toward them, showing her tiny knobs that were forming on it. "Wisteria," he mumbled with difficulty. "Beau-ti-ful soon."

She was pleased that she understood him perfectly. 79

It just took a little concentration and filling in the blanks. She was confident they'd be carrying on real conversations soon. "That would surprise me to see it beautiful, it surely would," she said. "I'd sure like to keep up with its progress, Mr. Billy—if you don't mind, that is."

Then Ginny Ruth helped Mr. Billy gather eggs, although she was scared half to death of the hens. But Mr. Billy showed her how he distracted them with feed while he collected the eggs.

"I don't know why I didn't think of that myself," she said. "And Cyrilla, why, she sure does it the hard way!" She was amazed that he managed somehow to get the eggs without breaking any and concluded that Mr. Billy had a personal guardian angel.

When that was done, Ginny Ruth helped Mr. Billy turn the red clay soil that would be their small vegetable garden. She helped him dip string into creosote, too, then lay it the length of the rows to be planted. That would keep the bugs away, and when there were plants, it would keep the deer and rabbits away. Mr. Billy struggled to explain to her that the animals feared the odor would overpower their sense of smell, that they would not be able to detect their enemies, and so they stayed away.

Ginny Ruth danced along the rows, dropping seeds into the troughs. She was singing a song that Paw had taught her, "One for the rook, one for the crow, one to die, and one to grow."

When she looked up Mr. Billy was smiling, and she giggled hysterically, feeling for a brief moment the giddiness she had felt with Paw.

She was dirty and her hands were covered with blisters. She drew water from the well, and they poured it over each other's hands to rinse off most of the dirt. But she still had angry red under her nails and caught in the pockets of bursting blisters.

The sun was setting behind the hills. Maw would be expecting her. Ginny Ruth had worked a long time, but she felt proud of herself for all she had accomplished. Mrs. Gaither gave her a small loaf of freshly baked bread as she left.

Maw, on seeing the bread, gave her what-for. "You can hardly pat yourself on the back for giving charitably if you took bread in exchange!" Maw told her.

Angrily Ginny Ruth held out her hands, indicating the blisters and few bruises. "I reckon I gave an inch off my hide that nobody paid for," she stormed. "And I didn't hurt nobody's pride by refusing a gift, neither."

She was surprised and pleased when Maw offered no further arguments. In silence they ate the mustard greens that had been left from the school lunch on Friday. Maw stubbornly ate the leftover cornbread, while Ginny Ruth munched contentedly on the fresh bread with a clear conscience.

On Monday the reverend aired the schoolroom of its smells of oil and chalk. And, in honor of a pretty fair temperature, Lester's asafetida bag was gone, mak- 81 ing the room quite tolerable. The students spent a portion of the day with the spring cleaning, washing the chalkboards, dusting the erasers, and making the room look clean and pleasant.

By the end of the day, Ginny Ruth was feeling a sense of renewed enthusiasm for life. She fell into step with Maw, who ordinarily left earlier but had stayed behind for her own spring cleaning in the kitchen.

As they passed the Simmses' house, Ginny Ruth chanced a quick glance in their direction. To her delighted surprise, Mrs. Simms's eyes were squarely and unquestionably following her movements. For a brief moment, their eyes met.

Flushing, the old woman quickly returned her attention to her garden.

"Ha!" Ginny Ruth squealed. "Caught ya! I caught you!" She did a little jig, spinning in half turns like a yearling first let out to pasture.

She caught a glimpse of Maw's face, frozen in fury. Maw said nothing, but the artery at her temple pulsed angrily, and Ginny Ruth knew that Maw was silently cursing that impish part of Paw in her.

But it couldn't spoil her moment. Her grandma had seen her, really seen her.

SEVEN

When she and Maw had reached their cabin, Ginny Ruth pulled up short, grabbing Maw's arm. Minute green sprigs were just beginning to push through the rust dirt near their door. "Oh, Maw, just imagine what they'll look like in a few weeks. Just like those magazine pictures!"

Maw's face was still too pinched with anger at Ginny Ruth to acknowledge the sprucing up the little flowers would do. Ginny Ruth knew it would be awhile before Maw could bring herself to forgive her daughter for reaching across the protective barriers she and the Simmses had drawn around themselves.

Still nothing could diminish her own joy of the moment. She squatted by the tiny sprigs, drinking in their fresh color with her eyes. She felt a smile creeping onto her face that refused to be contained, even when she went into the cabin, which was bleak in comparison to the awakening outdoors.

Maw was shoving pots and plates around on the shelf by the fireplace. "I need salt for tonight," she snapped. "And flour. And you see that Mr. Bob digs deep into 83 the barrel. I don't want no exposed flour, you hear?"

"Yes'm," Ginny Ruth said. She paused at the door to see the tiny sprigs once more, then skipped along the footpath toward the store.

When she stepped onto the store porch, Bob Ranger was just closing up. "Will it take long, Ginny Ruth?" he asked. "Annie's maw passed on just a few minutes ago. I got to get on home."

"Just some flour and salt, Mr. Bob. I am awfully sorry about Miss Annie's maw. I think maybe I better take a pound of them black-eyes, too. Maw'll want to be fixing them for the mourning."

Mr. Bob gathered the staples and peas hastily, then followed Ginny Ruth from the store. He turned a sign around to read CLOSED.

Ginny Ruth hurried back down the road, pausing only long enough to tell Mr. Billy about Mrs. Gilmer's passing and to scratch Scaredy Cat behind the ears. Mr. Billy shuffled on into the house to pass the word to his wife as Ginny Ruth ran home with the sad news.

"I picked up some black-eyed peas so's we could fix 'em for the mourning," she told Maw after she'd reported Mrs. Gilmer's death.

Maw stopped her stewing over Ginny Ruth's behavior with the Simmses. "You did right, Ginny Ruth. Fetch some onions from the patch," she told her. "They ain't full growed, but they'll flavor it some."

84   Maw cleaned and prepared the peas while Ginny

Ruth gathered the onions. When they were bubbling, the two of them went to bed early, knowing that the next day would be filled with the activities traditional to a death in Clemmons.

By the time Ginny Ruth and Maw arrived at the Gilmers' small house on the far side of the school, Miss Nettie was already well in control. Mr. Gilmer had passed on four years ago. Mrs. Gilmer had lived alone since then.

There wasn't a death, a wedding, or a birth that Miss Nettie Pritchert didn't choreograph. From the moment of the announcement, she bustled in like a general commanding his troops. And no one questioned her right or her authority to do so.

Mattresses leaned against the chicken-wire fence, airing in the light breeze that stirred. A few children policed the yard, and one hosed down the front porch.

School was always closed for a death, and for the younger children it was something of a holiday. The older ones, however, were expected to lend a hand to the bereaved.

"Get them curtains down for washing, Emma," Miss Nettie barked in her high-pitched, cawing voice. "Alma, pull the linens. Laurie, these here windows need a real going over."

Miss Nettie aimed her feather duster at each woman as she snapped off her commands. Her hair was tied up in a kerchief, her sleeves were rolled back, and her apron was in place. She was in total and unquestionable control.

Maw took her bowl of peas into the kitchen, placing them on the stove shelf to keep them warming.

"Polly, pull out them dishes and make 'em shine," Miss Nettie told Maw. "The flatware and glasses, too. There'll be plenty of folks here to eat."

Maw fell into her appointed duties without a word of argument, motioning for Ginny Ruth to help her. Ginny Ruth put a kettle of water on the stove to heat.

"That other daughter'll be dallying in here at the last minute, I suppose," Maw muttered half under her breath as she stacked the dishes in the pan.

That other daughter, Ginny Ruth figured, probably meant Miss Lilly, who had married a tractor salesman from Houston, where they now lived. Clemmons folks accused Miss Lilly of going "high tone" on them: Although her fancy car was seen at Mrs. Gilmer's often, Miss Lilly rarely visited anyone else during her trips to Clemmons.

Not that Ginny Ruth could blame her for avoiding them. "Tinted your hair," they'd say, as if she were consorting with the devil. "Too much rouge," they'd complain to one another. What was the use?

Ginny Ruth helped Maw pull the dishes from the shelf, wondering why it was necessary to clean dishes that were already clean and put away. Nobody questioned Miss Nettie's commands, though.

86   Miss Annie had arrived, but mostly she was tending

her small baby. The bereaved were not expected to participate in the cleanup.

The Reverend Trowbridge, his tall, thin frame slightly bent in an S shape, was murmuring to Miss Annie, asking her preference for church and graveside songs. Did she have any favorite Bible verses for him to read, and so on.

Lester came with word from the bank, where one of the few telephones was located, that Miss Lilly wouldn't be there until the following day. That meant an extra day off from school, Ginny Ruth figured. But it also meant, thanks to Miss Nettie, more washing and cooking than this house had seen in a dozen years.

Almost as if on cue, Miss Nettie sighed her martyr's sigh and announced, "Well, this gives us a bit more time to tidy up proper, although it will put a strain on Annie."

Miss Alma and Miss Emma retreated to the washtub outside, struggling together with the bulky curtains. Miss Laurie rubbed furiously at the living-room windows with a foul-smelling potion until they squeaked clean.

"Ginny Ruth," Miss Nettie barked, "help Laurie, or we'll never be through before the body gets back from Stallings."

Ginny Ruth shivered slightly. Yesterday it was Mrs. Gilmer. Now it was "the body," as if she didn't have a name. The custom in Clemmons was to keep the body lying at the family home until it was buried. 87

Ginny Ruth had heard that in lots of towns the body stayed at the funeral home, although that seemed kind of cold and unfriendly to her.

It was far more practical to have Mrs. Gilmer right there in Clemmons, where folks could pay their proper respects. Most folks wouldn't be able to go all the way into Stallings to the funeral home. It also saved the family the added expense of a funeral chapel. Practical reasons aside, it was tradition now, and Clemmons folks stood firm on tradition.

Ginny Ruth grabbed a rag from the pile Miss Laurie had gathered. She dipped into the liquid and began working on the middle window. The solution dribbled down her arms to her elbows, and then onto the floor.

"Wring out that rag, girl!" Miss Nettie snapped. "Lord 'a' mercy, were you raised in a cow pasture?"

Miss Nettie groaned suddenly, flushing because she'd called on the Lord just as the Reverend Trowbridge had returned to the living room.

Obviously flustered, she patted her apron, adjusted her kerchief, and fluttered her eyes briefly, flashing a warm smile in his direction. "Would you like a cup of coffee, Reverend?" she asked. "You know, my coffee brew is practically world famous."

The Reverend Trowbridge backed off slightly, his face flushed, his eyes darting nervously from side to side like a trapped raccoon looking for an escape from the dogs. "I—I bow to your reputation for coffee making, Miss Nettie," he said. "But I must see to it that the church is properly attired for the funeral tomorrow."

His outstretched hand touched the doorknob, and the good reverend whirled and was out the door in one swoop. Once again he'd foiled Miss Nettie's attempt to convince him that she'd make a perfect second Mrs. Trowbridge, Ginny Ruth noticed with no small amusement.

No doubt satisfied that he was out of earshot, Miss Nettie heaved a quick sigh. Then she read off another list of duties for her clean-up battalion.

The food was arriving more frequently by noon. Mrs. Gaither brought a fried chicken. Elvira brought over a baked hen and her mama's apologies because she'd given birth to Imogene and couldn't attend to any of the chores.

Before the day was over there were biscuits, loaves of bread, turnovers, and pies in the keeper. Chicken, a side of smoked bacon, and a variety of vegetables were stacked one on top of the other on the stove shelf. It was hard to believe that Clemmons was steeped in poverty when so much food materialized for a passing. But everyone no doubt sacrificed at home to make that generous showing at the mourning.

It seemed to Ginny Ruth that a funeral was only an excuse for eating. For every morsel people brought, they "didn't mind at all" if they had "just a dab o' that   89

apple pie" or "just a nibble of that there chicken," so
that a passing turned into more of an eating gala than
a mourning.

The Gaithers had volunteered to sit up with the
body. Maw had volunteered herself and Ginny Ruth,
who had no say in the matter at all. Although Ginny
Ruth had been spared this ritual of death before, Maw
figured she was plenty old enough to fulfill her "proper"
responsibilities now. Ginny Ruth groaned as Maw told
her.

"What for, Maw?" Ginny Ruth said. "Ain't nobody
gonna steal her. And she won't be going nowhere on
her own."

"Ginny Ruth!" Maw snapped. "Watch your mouth,
missy. It's proper that someone do it. And we'll be
here. And that's all there is to it."

Miss Nettie, no doubt tired from mule-flogging all
day, left shortly before dusk. Only Maw, Ginny Ruth,
and the Gaithers remained.

Dodson's Funeral Home had brought the embalmed
body back from Stallings, along with some black arm-
bands for the family and a fresh supply of palmetto
fans for the home and church. "Compliments of Dodson's Funeral Home," they said.

The casket was arranged at one end of the living
room with a magnificent spray of red roses that had
been sent by Miss Lilly and her husband. Only one
light burned in the room.

90   The freshly washed and ironed curtains rippled

slightly from the light breeze that blew through the window. Ginny Ruth noticed with dismay that all her scrubbing and rubbing on those windows had been unnecessary, since they were covered with the curtains anyway.

Kitchen chairs were brought in to provide more seating. Ginny Ruth sat on one, her legs entwined around its spool-shaped legs. She shifted slightly, making the chair squeak. Maw shot her a frown.

Ginny Ruth tried counting the roses in the spray, and moved on to the squares of the crocheted coverlet draped over the threadbare sofa, counting them forward and backward. Next she tried to imagine animals from the shapes of the leak stains on the ceiling. When she had exhausted those games, she tried to trace the stitches in her dress.

The cuckoo clock behind her suddenly sprang into action, and the little bird flung open its doors and pushed to the end of its spring. Ginny Ruth counted cuckoos. Only 8 P.M. All night to go, and she was already exhausted.

"How come Miss Annie ain't sitting up? It's her maw," Ginny Ruth whispered to Maw.

"She's too frail. Now hush up and act your age," Maw mouthed back at her. Ginny Ruth noticed a slight smile play over Mr. Billy's lips, or was it only that twitch? Drool in the corner of his mouth and on his chin was illuminated in the dim light.

The front porch creaked as someone stepped up. 91

The Schumans, who lived down near the river, tiptoed inside clumsily, futilely trying to make as little noise as possible. Mrs. Schuman, her tousled yellow ringlets crowning a round, pink face, nodded and walked over to where the Gaithers and Maw sat.

Mr. Schuman acknowledged them with a quick nod. Then he moved to the dark corner, where he stood uncomfortably trying to find a place for his hands, finally hooking his thumbs over his coverall straps.

"Mrs. Gilmer looked plumb awful when I last seen her," Mrs. Schuman said in a whisper that could have called pigs to the trough. "I just knowed her time on this earth was gone. Awful. Just awful."

She tiptoed over to stand by the casket, clucking and shaking her head from side to side. She bowed her head solemnly for a moment, then turned briskly back to the living with a slight sigh that sounded more like relief that a necessary duty had been done.

"My, but don't she look pretty?" Mrs. Schuman said, forgetting to whisper. "The picture of health. So natural!"

Ginny Ruth wrinkled her face, turning to see the reaction of the others. If they saw anything illogical about Mrs. Schuman's observations, they gave no indication of it whatsoever.

Maw nodded solemnly. "Yes, it's a shame. A real shame. But she's in her glory now."

Ginny Ruth sighed wearily. Mrs. Schuman seemed

to take notice of her for the first time. Pinching her cheek, she said, "Stand up, girl, and let me take a look at you!"

Maw jabbed at Ginny Ruth, who was cringing against the hard-backed chair. "Stand up," she whispered.

Her cheek still stinging from the pinch, Ginny Ruth reluctantly pulled to her feet. She was aware that her toes protruded from her sandals even more than they had a week ago.

"Lawd, how she has growed!" Mrs. Schuman said. "Why, I bet you got yourself a feller, ain't ya?" She pinched Ginny Ruth again, this time on both cheeks.

Ginny Ruth flopped back into the chair, her face burning and blood red and her feelings running from anger to embarrassment and back again. "No'm," she replied. "I'm too young for fellers."

Mrs. Schuman's voice rose another octave. "You're joshing! Why, Jimmy John and me was courtin' by the time I was your size." She patted her ample chest and nodded toward Ginny Ruth's only slightly developed one. "Sure enough, weren't we, Jimmy John?"

Mr. Schuman shifted his hands to his pockets and cleared his throat. Ginny Ruth pressed herself against the chair, praying it would swallow her up.

"You tell Miss Annie that we were here now. And I suppose Miss Lilly will come sashaying in here tomorrow. See y'all at the burying," she said, pushing through the squeaking door and onto the porch. Mr. Schuman followed a few steps behind, pausing only to nod his farewells to them.

"Stop gritting your teeth, Ginny Ruth," Maw said. "That is most annoying."

"So's calling attention to my . . ." She glanced over to see that Mr. Billy wasn't looking, then finished in a whisper, "my personals."

Maw's mouth twitched slightly. Ginny Ruth wasn't sure if she almost smiled or not.

Mr. Billy pushed from his chair and muttered something to Mrs. Gaither, then went onto the front porch. Ginny Ruth followed him with her eyes. She heard the squeak of the porch swing as he sank into it and pushed.

"Why don't you go with him, child?" Mrs. Gaither said. "It's going to be a long night."

Ginny Ruth glanced toward Maw to see an affirmative nod, then hurried out before Maw could change her mind. Mr. Billy stopped the swing, and she sat on the slatted seat beside him. The light from the living room threw a filtered orange glow on them.

"Mr. Billy, do you ever wonder what hell might be like? I mean, I don't think there's really a fire at all, do you? I think maybe it is really red dust. I think God must've created two Clemmonses. One he called hell. Don't you?"

94   Mr. Billy's arm jerked as he lifted it to touch her

hair. His eyes reflected in the light, and Ginny Ruth felt they must be open windows to his innermost thoughts. If only she could unlock their secrets.

"Kin-dred spi-rits," he muttered.

She was glad that he remembered the poem. Ginny Ruth felt warmed by his touch, as shaky and uncontrolled as it was. Paw used to touch her hair. He wouldn't say anything, just touch it and smile at her, and she felt so loved. Suddenly she grabbed his hand and tried to hold it still for him. "Does it hurt, Mr. Billy? Does the shaking hurt you?"

"Ex-haust-ing," he said. "So—tired."

"How could God do this to you, Mr. Billy?"

His eyes clouded slightly, disappointment coloring them. "Not—God," he mumbled. "Cow."

"Do you hate that cow, Mr. Billy? Never mind, Mr. Billy. I know you don't. Hate just ain't in your soul, is it? It's mine that is black with anger. Maybe I'd 'a' been better off if I'd never read any of Miss Marnie's books about such wonderful places and people, if I'd never knowed the happy times my paw brought. If I didn't know any better—"

Mr. Billy frowned. "Your heart—always knew. Eagle—among—sparrows. But you—your words—can help sparrows—soar like eagles."

Ginny Ruth echoed his words, trying to absorb and understand them. "An eagle?"

"You help me stand, walk right—inside. Here—and   95

here." He touched his head and his heart.

His words encircled her like a protective cloak. Tears welled and spilled down her cheeks.

She tried to say something, but the words stuck in her throat. As she returned to the living room, her step was light. She felt as if she could fly like an eagle.

Inside Ginny Ruth leaned her head against the high wooden back of the chair and closed her eyes. The room faded from sight, and she was standing in wildflowers at her doorstep. She and Paw were dancing around and around. They had eagles' wings on their backs, and they were laughing and hugging and singing. Only somehow Mr. Billy's face got all mixed up with Paw's and she knew something was wrong, but she couldn't sort it out.

"Ginny Ruth," Maw said, shaking her shoulder. "Wake up."

She blinked slowly as the morning light startled her puffy eyes. Her body was stiff and sore and bore the pattern of the chair. Somehow she had managed to sleep through the night without waking.

"Go wash your face," Maw said. "Folks'll be arriving soon."

Mrs. Gaither was frying bacon and eggs. Mr. Billy balanced precariously on a stool, retrieving a jar of jelly from the top shelf.

Miss Annie, Mr. Bob, and the baby arrived as the breakfast was being turned onto a platter. The whole

cook-eat-and-wash-up routine had begun again.

It was around ten in the morning when Miss Lilly and her husband, Nester Fuller, drove up in a shiny, ivory-colored Ford sedan. The car was so free of red dust that Ginny Ruth was positive they had stopped at the river to clean it up before driving into town. Ginny Ruth gawked at Miss Lilly, who'd assumed an air of glamour since she'd moved to Houston. She hardly looked kin to the frail, cotton-garbed Annie.

Miss Lilly was dressed in a dark faille dress with silk stockings and patent leather pumps. A pheasant feather bobbed saucily on her matching hat, and, although the weather was to be fairly hot, around her neck was a small fur collar held in place with a brooch that was probably made of real diamonds. Her hair was lighter and her lashes darker, and she was rouged and powdered and smelled like fresh flowers.

Mr. Nester had a broad smile, which he flashed readily. Ginny Ruth could see how he'd charm anyone into buying one of his tractors, whether they had the money or not. A diamond on his finger caught the sunlight through the window. Never before had Ginny Ruth seen jewelry on a man.

She stared open-mouthed at the spectacle the two of them made in their fine clothes and jewelry. Mr. Nester smiled at Ginny Ruth, causing her to shrink against Maw and to feel awkward and plain.

She wasn't the only one who felt that way. The Fullers got more attention at the funeral than the late Mrs. Gilmer. Clemmons folks solemnly marched up to view the body, once it had been moved to the church for the service. But on the way back to their pews they walked more slowly, gawking openly at the Fullers, who sat resplendent in the front pew, right next to the withered-looking Annie and her family.

The procession walked the dusty block to the shady cemetery. Only the late Mrs. Gilmer rode.

At the graveside, Miss Lilly pulled a lace-decorated handerchief from her purse and wiped the red dust from her patent shoes. She wrinkled her nose at the soiled handkerchief, flicking it into her purse with a slight shudder.

As was the custom in Clemmons, when the preacher had read a few words over the grave, the family and friends each stepped forward and scooped a handful of dirt into the grave. Miss Lilly frowned and stepped back, refusing to take part.

Miss Annie, clutching her baby to her with one arm, stooped to fling two handfuls into the grave, obviously one for her sister. Ginny Ruth leaned closer, squinting at Miss Lilly. Now Miss Lilly didn't look so glamorous. And even if she had escaped her poverty, she hadn't escaped her ignorance. Ginny Ruth sniffed piously. She would never be like Miss Lilly.

Despite the Fullers' obvious relative wealth, their greed apparently had gone unquenched. When the day was over, they left Clemmons in their shiny little Ford, well laden with "mementos" that had been claimed by

the fair Lilly with little regard for Annie's needs.

Ginny Ruth helped Maw and Miss Nettie stack away the remaining dishes, replace the kitchen chairs, then close the house. It was quiet, except for the ticking of the cuckoo clock, which would soon wind down and be silent.

Suddenly it hit Ginny Ruth. That poor old lady was gone. Ginny Ruth tried to shrug it off. Rural folks learned it sooner than city folks, maybe; death was a part of life.

As she and Maw walked toward home, each lost in her own thoughts, Ginny Ruth looked back at the sun sinking slowly behind the hill. It was a glowing orange ball and looked as if it were reflecting the rust dirt.

Below it she saw the pines, dark green and heavily shadowed now, stretching toward the orange ball. The clouds were pink and purple with bright golden borders.

Words ran through her mind: Dark green fingers, reaching to touch the gilt-edged clouds, to snare them, to trap them forever. But clouds can no more be trapped than dreams.

Ginny Ruth watched as the orange ball turned into a small eyebrow, then disappeared. The sky became lavender, then purple. Mr. Billy had said her words could help him stand and walk right inside, that she could help sparrows soar like eagles. She smiled, imagining herself as an eagle rising, turning across that sky, beckoning to the sparrows to follow.

EIGHT

With the spring planting at hand, school attendance dropped considerably. The students who remained were subjected to the reverend's hellfire-and-damnation speeches whenever they got a mite out of hand. Ginny Ruth figured the burr under his blanket was that the eligible ladies of Clemmons had tired of waiting for his mourning period to end and had declared open war for his hand.

The Davis girls did their part to keep the good reverend in a state of what he called "righteous indignation." Given to fits of giggles, which they blamed on spring, they often filled every corner of the room, their faces turned to the walls.

The real problem, though, was Miss Nettie, who'd taken to dropping by the school at lunchtime or after classes "to do my part in helping out." Usually she had just baked some little tidbit that she brought along for "Reverend Amos," as she now called him with a fluttering of her eyelashes.

100   In the lunchroom Ginny Ruth nudged Cyrilla and

nodded toward the door, where Miss Nettie was marching in with a still-steaming peach cobbler. "It'd serve 'em right if they wound up with each other," she whispered to Cyrilla, who managed to stifle a snicker and save herself from a corner of the cafeteria. The reverend didn't allow more than whispered conversation during meals. He said noise bothered his digestion, although Ginny Ruth couldn't imagine anything disturbing that.

It appeared to Ginny Ruth that the reverend was beginning to weaken. Greedily he folded his thin body onto one of the benches and put away half a cobbler while Miss Nettie fluttered about him like a bird after a worm. She straightened the collar of her dress and patted her hair a dozen times, all the while chattering into his ear. He nodded in agreement but never stopped chewing.

Soon the newness of the courting wore off and the children hardly noticed her pursuit, being only slightly more aware of it than the reverend himself.

After school every day, Ginny Ruth visited the Gaithers and did odd jobs for Mr. Billy. Sometimes they did nothing but sit on the front porch, watching Scaredy Cat's antics. Sometimes Ginny Ruth closed her eyes and pretended it was Paw there with her, not that frail, quaking old man, though she had learned to overlook his physical appearance and managed to understand most of what he was saying.

One afternoon Ginny Ruth stopped dumbfounded at the gate, staring. The gnarled old gray vine she had   101 wanted to cut down was profuse with clusters of lavender flowers that hung grapelike.

"I'll declare, Mr. Billy," she said, hurrying to his side. "If that ain't the most beautiful sight in the whole wide world, I don't know what is!"

She pulled a cluster toward her nose. "They smell as pretty as they look," she said. "It just seems real unnatural for a thing without a single green leaf to be so all-fired decorated, don't it? But then I guess it must be natural, or it wouldn't be there, would it?"

Ginny Ruth realized she talked too much around Mr. Billy, but she felt obligated to hold up both ends of the conversation. She wished she felt comfortable with the silence. Maybe that would come later.

He made an awkward gesture and spoke in a slurred, slow sentence, "Ginny—Ruth—write poem."

"A poem? You want me to write a poem about that vine? Why, I'll think on it awhile, Mr. Billy. I'll sure try."

Awkwardly he touched her cheek. Then, obviously embarrassed, he jerked his hand away.

She brought her hand to the spot where he'd touched her. "Paw used to touch my cheek that way."

Mr. Billy frowned, trying to form words.

Figuring he meant to apologize, Ginny Ruth hastily added, "It's nice, Mr. Billy. I . . . I miss my paw so much."

A wave of relief engulfed her. She'd never really said

that aloud to anyone but Maw. Somehow, saying it aloud, admitting that he was really gone, she felt a burden lift a bit. It wasn't a smaller burden now, just an easier one to carry.

"Molasses cookies in the keep!" Mrs. Gaither called.

When they had eaten a few cookies, Ginny Ruth brushed the crumbs off Mr. Billy into her hand and flung them out the back screen door to the ever-waiting chickens. Then she followed him to the rolltop desk in the living room, where they were going to begin straightening an assortment of photos and certificates into an album.

"It'll probably take weeks, Mr. Billy," she warned. "I could work some Saturdays, too. But the little time after school won't help much, I'm afraid."

Mrs. Gaither, mending some socks as she rocked, chuckled. "All that stuff has been piling up since we first married. I don't reckon a few more weeks will make much difference one way or the other."

There were pictures of the Gaithers when they were very young. Ginny Ruth stared at them, realizing that Mr. Billy hadn't had all that wretched shaking then, that at one time he'd been as strong as Paw.

She dabbed some glue onto the back of the photo and pressed it to a clean page. Mr. Billy sat nearby, his hands shaking too badly to help.

Ginny Ruth ran her fingers over the array of photos, trying to see which might come next in the order of 103 time. Her hand touched one, then another, as she glanced back for his approval.

He shook his head until she touched one, then nodded sadly that it was next. Ginny Ruth looked at the picture. The Gaithers were holding a little baby and smiling so proudly they looked as if they'd burst right out of the picture.

There was but one other picture of the three of them that she found among those fading old photographs. They were squatting on the ground, and a toddler girl was braced between them, her chubby little cheeks dimpled in a big smile.

Ginny Ruth glanced back at Mr. Billy. In his eyes she saw a sadness she had not seen before. She dared not ask and risk bringing the hurt even more to the surface. But she could guess. They'd lost their only child to either an accident or an illness. What a wonderful father he would have been to a girl. Kind, encouraging. Surely that little girl would have loved him back, even if other kids did make fun of him.

"That glue is gonna dry on the brush, child," Mrs. Gaither said. "I think maybe your mind isn't on that old album."

Ginny Ruth snapped to attention. She dabbed the glue onto the back of the photograph and pressed it into the album. "Sorry," she said. "Just thinking."

"Don't apologize for thinking, child," Mrs. Gaither said. "It wouldn't hurt any of us to do it every now
and then."

As Ginny Ruth stirred the photographs, her fingers touched some coins. "Goodness, Mr. Billy, don't you believe in banks?" she joked. "You got a whole bunch of money— Why, this ain't real money."

He held out his hand, and she steadied it long enough to clasp his fingers around one of the coins. "Ger—Ger-man," he said.

Ginny Ruth took back the coin and scrutinized it. "Is that where you were in the army, Mr. Billy? In Germany?" She opened one of the little drawers of the rolltop desk and put the coins inside.

Glancing at the mantel clock, Ginny Ruth jumped up. "I better be getting myself home before Maw gives me what-for."

She rose to leave, but Mr. Billy clumsily pulled her back, muttering something she didn't understand. He rummaged awkwardly through his pockets and brought out three dimes.

"Take them, child," Mrs. Gaither said. "Billy wants you to have them. You've been working so hard these past weeks."

"But I can't!" Ginny Ruth said. "I wasn't working for no money. Honest!"

Mr. Billy nodded jerkily. "Ice-cream—ice-cream cone."

"Don't deny us the pleasure of doing something for you," Mrs. Gaither said.

In a sudden burst of gratitude, Ginny Ruth hugged them both and hurried home. She tucked the dimes 105 in her pocket as she approached the cabin. If Maw knew she would insist that Ginny Ruth put them in the offering plate Sunday or save them for something special or, even worse, make her take them back.

No, sir, Ginny Ruth decided. Maw just didn't seem to understand that other folks needed to give sometimes, to feel good about themselves. Mr. Billy would feel just awful if she gave back the dimes.

She knelt by the cabin door to examine her flowers. They were growing swiftly. Some of them had little knobs like the ones on the wisteria vine before it bloomed. Soon she'd have blooms at her doorstep, too, just like the ones in the magazine pictures.

That evening she and Maw ate the leftovers from the school lunch: sauerkraut, sausages, and cornbread. Although sauerkraut twice in one day was twice too often for Ginny Ruth, she ate every drop, keeping her mind on the money instead of her slimy food.

When they had washed up, Ginny Ruth slipped into her bunk, rummaging through her mind for images that could be used in a poem about the wisteria vine. It was like a sleeping beauty that had looked dead all winter. And now from that dead thing had come this beautiful profusion of color. She herself would have considered it hopeless, even pulled it up. But Mr. Billy had had the faith to wait, and it had rewarded him with its beauty.

106   Her lids fluttered closed as she considered it. Yes,

she decided as she drifted into sleep, it was Mr. Billy's faith that had touched the vine and made it beautiful. Remembering his Christmas visit, she smiled. Maybe his faith had touched her and would make her beautiful, too.

The next day in the schoolyard, Cyrilla whispered an invitation to Ginny Ruth. "We're going fishing Saturday. Really it's an excuse to see the yarb woman. You have just got to go with us. Oh, please, please!" she implored.

The Reverend Trowbridge said that the yarb woman's mixtures were sorcery. He said folks should go to medical doctors instead. Maybe he said that because his brother was a doctor in Stallings. But plenty of the grown-ups went secretly to get her blends of herbs and curatives. Maw, of course, had never been there. She said the yarb woman was a tool of the devil and she heated her medicines on brimstone.

Ginny Ruth wanted to go, and her heart quickened at the thought of seeing the yarb woman for herself. But she shook her head vigorously. "Can't," she said. "I got something else to do."

Cyrilla put her hands on her hips. "With Mr. Billy, I suppose! First it was Miss Marnie. I could kinda understand that, what with y'all having so much in common, waiting for someone and all. But now that weird old man! What's the matter with you anyway, Ginny Ruth? You hang around that crazy old man all 107 the time. If you're looking for a new paw, you could find somebody better than him!"

Ginny Ruth felt fire build up inside. She shoved Cyrilla with a force that sent them both tumbling to the ground. She grabbed a handful of Cyrilla's hair on both sides. "You take that back!" Ginny Ruth snarled at her.

"Ow!" Cyrilla screamed as the others gathered around them. "Let go my hair!"

"I got a paw, and I ain't looking for another one," Ginny Ruth screamed. "And besides, I'm a hired hand at the Gaithers'. It ain't nothing else." She had a sudden flash of the reverend's Easter sermon, when he talked about Peter denying the Lord and the cock crowing. Her stomach did a flip-flop. She let go of Cyrilla's hair and stood up.

Cyrilla, her lip slightly pouting, got up and brushed off her dress and patted her hair back into place. "Hired hand, my foot!" she growled. "Everybody's talkin'. It ain't natural."

Ginny Ruth fought to control the rage churning inside. She looked at the faces of the others standing in a circle, watching the argument. Their expressions were clear. They all thought she was a fool for hanging around Mr. Billy. She jerked the dimes from her pocket and held them out so the sun reflected on them. "See? I got my wages yesterday right here. And I aim to spend them on an ice-cream cone this very afternoon."

108   Cyrilla stopped scowling at Ginny Ruth. Cocking

her head, she eyed the coins greedily. In a family as big as the Davises', store-bought ice cream was as rare a treat as it was for Ginny Ruth. "A cone? What flavor?"

Ginny Ruth straightened her shoulders. She knew she had everyone's admiration now. "I don't rightly know. I'm going to take my time deciding. And I ain't gonna be influenced by outsiders, either."

The reverend rang the bell for the children to return to the classroom. Ginny Ruth dusted off her dress, grateful that he hadn't heard the ruckus in the play yard. If he had they'd be in for another sermon. Now, if word didn't reach Maw in the kitchen, she'd be home free!

She couldn't help but feel a bit funny about her exchange with Cyrilla, though. Why had she reacted so strongly to her? Was she mad about the slur against Paw? Or against Mr. Billy?

She and Cyrilla had their differences—more than ever, lately—but they were still friends. While the reverend was writing on the chalkboard, Ginny Ruth hastily passed a note to Cyrilla, promising her a lick if she happened to see her. Of course, Ginny Ruth had no intention of seeing her if she could help it!

After school Ginny Ruth counted the dimes a half-dozen times as she walked toward the drugstore, anticipating the grand moment. She pushed through the screen door, and the bell jangled merrily above her head. It was as heavenly as any angel's trumpet to her ear.

Immediately she felt the cool stir of air from the ceiling fans that rotated slowly. She ran her fingers along the marble-topped counter that felt cool to her touch.

Ginny Ruth moved down the counter where the jars of licorice, buttons, jawbreakers, and peppermint sticks were temptingly displayed. She stopped to admire each jar and study its contents.

She stepped onto the brass rail, boosting herself onto the high, leather-covered stool. She pushed against the counter so that the wobbly stool made a full turn and she was again seeing herself in the big beveled mirror at the back of the fountain.

Mr. Booker, the pharmacist and owner, came from the back, tying on his white apron as he spoke. "Why, Ginny Ruth! This is a nice surprise."

She licked her lips in anticipation. "I'd like to see a menu," she told him, feeling that she'd nearly burst with pride. She dropped her coins on the counter with a clink to show him she had the money.

Ginny Ruth studied the menu. There were sodas and colas and malteds, all too expensive. "You don't mention here what cone flavors you got, Mr. Booker," she said.

"Strawberry, chocolate, and vanilla, as always," he said. "I also got orange sherbet."

Mentally she tasted each one, remembering what it was like. "I ain't ever had orange sherbet," she confessed. "Does it taste anything like real oranges? I had me some of them last Christmas."

He scratched his chin. "Well, to tell you the truth, it don't have quite the real flavor to me. As for the ice cream, you get three dips anyway, and it wouldn't be too much trouble to dip one of each, if you don't favor any particular one."

"Oh, lordy mercy!" Ginny Ruth said. "That sounds deliciously piggish. I think I'll do just that. Thank you for the suggestion, Mr. Booker!"

She watched as Mr. Booker reached into a jar with a paper napkin and in one expert twist wound it around the stem of a double cone.

He pulled the silver scoop from its holder, dipping it into water. As he flung open the vanilla cannister, the sweet smell wafted up, teasing Ginny Ruth's nose. She inhaled, licking her lips. He dipped the scoop again, this time into the chocolate, which he placed on the other side of the double cone. It had a more piquant smell, she observed.

"And now!" he said, flipping back the cover from the strawberry ice cream. He settled the pink ball on top, pushing to secure it.

Ginny Ruth inhaled again, fully believing that she could float away on the delicious smell. She counted out the three dimes, and in a grand and sweeping gesture, Mr. Booker handed her the triple-decker cone.

He seemed to be enjoying the trade as much as she. **111**

He pushed the sale key on the brass cash register, and the drawer popped out with a snappy ring. The dimes clinked into the drawer, one at a time.

Ginny Ruth reached out her tongue, running it along the strawberry. That dear Mr. Billy, making it possible for her to enjoy such a treat! "Oh, lordy, heaven must surely be paved with this," she said, trying not to swallow it but to allow it to melt in her mouth so the taste would remain longer.

Ginny Ruth caught sight of herself in the mirror. It doubled the pleasure to observe and to eat at the same time.

The bell above the door jangled, and Ginny Ruth turned to see Alpha, Beta, Cyrilla, Daniel, and Elvira all standing there in lip-licking expectancy.

Her heart tightened in her chest. She slid down from the stool and went to meet them, grateful that Francie, Grace, Hester, and Imogene were not the traveling age!

NINE

Still feeling a bit guilty about her attack on Cyrilla—and a real curiosity about the yarb woman—Ginny Ruth suggested that Saturday would be a good day to add catfish to their meager menu. Maw, despite her distrust of the rambunctious Davis girls, yielded to the tasty temptation and allowed Ginny Ruth to go fishing.

"I thought you were working with Mr. Billy," Maw reminded her.

Ginny Ruth swallowed the hard lump that threatened to choke her. "I reckon I can work on that old album of his any Saturday. But catfish ain't gonna wait." She scooted outside and to the back of the cabin before Maw could ask any more questions, cautiously neglecting to mention the impending visit to the yarb woman.

Ginny Ruth retrieved her bamboo pole from its shelf in back and checked to see that her hook and float were still intact. She patted her pocket to be sure she had her small chunk of Ivory Soap, which softened in the water and attracted catfish better than any other bait.

The Davis girls were waiting where the path and the road crossed. "You know," Ginny Ruth suggested, still feeling a pang of remorse about not going to the Gaithers' as she'd promised, "it'd be right neighborly of us if we asked Mr. Billy to go with us."

"Are you crazy?" Cyrilla asked. "Why, that old coot would scare all the fish away with his silly shaking. Besides, he'd tell on us about the yarb woman."

"He ain't no old coot, and he ain't no snitch," Ginny Ruth muttered, half under her breath. "He's kind and—"

Cyrilla did a quick imitation of Mr. Billy's rubbery-legged walk, and her sisters took up the imitation, giggling as they did.

Ginny Ruth closed her mouth tightly, lest her lips open and let angry words escape.

They reached the corner of the Gaithers' property, and Ginny Ruth stared at her feet as the rust-red dirt sifted through her toes. She clutched her fishing pole and kept walking, pretending she didn't see Mr. Billy sitting on the porch swing, waiting, just as he did every Saturday, for her to come.

Cyrilla broke into the imitation ever so briefly and the Davis sisters started to giggle. Ginny Ruth stared straight ahead. She heard the screen door squeak shut. Oh, lordy, she thought, was that only Scaredy Cat whining to go with her, or was that a cock crowing a second time?

After all, she consoled herself, she wasn't any kin to

him, and she hadn't done any of the mocking herself. And it was her life, wasn't it? If she wanted to write about people and life, she had to experience some of it, didn't she?

If that were so, why did she feel as if she were carrying a hundred-pound conscience just then? Knowing Mr. Billy would understand didn't lighten her burden in the least.

After lagging behind, Ginny Ruth hurried to catch up to the girls. They were almost at the edge of Main Street, where the only patch of what passed as a sidewalk was located in front of the post office, bank, and drugstore.

The menfolk, blessed with fewer chores on Saturday, draped themselves along its length, deciding the fate of the weather, the crops, and the nation, while their women took care of unimportant details, like shopping and banking. They usually leaned in a semicircle against the red brick building, one foot drawn up behind them to balance. One hand held a paper wrapper, and the other deftly tapped tobacco from a small muslin sack. In a single move, a man could draw the sack shut with his teeth while rolling the paper around the tobacco between fingers and thumb. He would finish it off by licking the paper to seal it closed.

It had been the same as long as Ginny Ruth could remember. The Clemmons men never bothered with those fancier packaged cigarettes. Most preferred to make their own, even if they were clumsier, although 115 a few had taken to "chawing tobacco." Ginny Ruth closed her eyes, pretending for a minute that Paw was there with them, rolling his cigarettes.

"Lookee who's goin' fishin'," Lester's voice cut through. There were a few general snickers among the others, indicating that they doubted the girls' aptitude for catching fish.

Ginny Ruth narrowed her eyes at Lester, but she spoke loudly enough for the benefit of the rest of them, too. "You just entertain yourselves here all day, if you want. You can help us count the fish when we get back."

She, Cyrilla, Alpha, Beta, and Daniel walked as haughtily as they could as they crossed the highway to reach the path to the river.

Cautiously they tramped through the woods, doing quick steps when their bare feet met with a nettle or stone. It always took a bit of summer toughening before the feet could be comfortably bare after the winter's tendering process. But Ginny Ruth was so grateful to be out of the pinching sandals that she paid no attention to the discomfort.

The sun filtered through the tall pines, and a slight breeze ruffled the trees. The smell of moist, rotting leaves tickled Ginny Ruth's nose. She sneezed.

"Watch out for rattlers," Alpha warned. "They're out of hybernation by now."

"Yeah," Cyrilla said, snickering. "You can still catch
116   sight of remnants of Aunt Prissy's petticoats out here

from when a snake and her tangled on a picnic."

A rabbit, its ears pink from the sun, hopped across the path. To their right a frog croaked. Somewhere on the left another answered.

"That seems like a good spot," Daniel suggested when they reached a bend in the river that was near the footpath. They settled down to straighten their lines and bait their hooks.

"Oh, durn!" Alpha blurted. "The hook's caught in my dress."

"Be careful," Beta cautioned her. "That'll be my dress next year. And I'm tired of wearing your old patched-up stuff."

"Shush!" Cyrilla warned. "You'll scare the fish away."

They lowered their voices to whispers but barely slowed down their chatter. Ginny Ruth sat cross-legged on a pine-needle cushion she had made for herself, watching the float on her line as it bobbed gently with the ripples. "Why are we going to see the yarb woman?" she asked in a whisper. "Is somebody sick?"

Beta giggled. "Yeah, lovesick. We're going to get one of them love potions for Alpha."

"Alpha?" Ginny Ruth echoed. "But I thought she and James were already pretty sweet on each other."

Alpha sighed audibly. "He'll be home tomorrow. And I don't want to take any chances."

Cyrilla giggled. "Alpha figures before James goes back to camp this time, they'll be promised. That is, 117 if those love potions the yarb woman cooks up really work."

Ginny Ruth's float disappeared below the water's surface with a loud pop. She gave a quick yank on her pole. Something yanked back. "I got one!" she shrieked. "I got one!" She pulled the pole back quickly, and a squirming catfish flopped onto the bank behind her. The Davis sisters gathered around, leaping and squealing.

"Oh, lordy," Ginny Ruth cautioned. "Watch out for them whiskers. They'll sting the devil out of you."

She reached out to grab the fish behind the gills and carefully pulled the hook from its mouth. Cyrilla filled the bucket with river water, and Ginny Ruth dropped the catfish into the bucket.

"I always feel just a little bit sad when I catch something," Ginny Ruth said. She managed, however, to overcome her reluctance and again dipped her pole into the river. The Davis girls settled back with their poles, too. Before noon they'd managed to catch a fish each, and Ginny Ruth had caught a second. Already she was planning to drop off the biggest one at the Gaithers'.

She felt bad about not being there as she'd promised, and even worse about not acknowledging Mr. Billy's presence on the porch. She was hating herself just a little for letting the girls get away with mocking him. The sound of the door shutting haunted her. She could 118 just imagine the hurt on his face.

Alpha pulled out a kerchief full of buttered biscuits with jam for them to snack on. Lazily they nibbled and watched the rippling water.

"River's gettin' too warm," Cyrilla observed. "The fish are going to be staying at the bottom now. We might as well quit."

"We need to get on to the yarb woman anyway," Beta reminded them. "We have to support young love." She grinned broadly at Alpha, who tried to prove her maturity by shrugging off the teasing.

The girls pulled in their poles, carefully putting their hooks into the cork floats. Two at a time they took turns carrying the fish-laden bucket.

The yarb woman lived in a shack with a tin roof. It was about a half mile down the winding river that snaked through the tall pines. While no one confessed going to see the yarb woman, the path to her shack looked well-worn.

"This bucket is getting powerful heavy," Ginny Ruth complained. "This just ain't going to work, carrying it all the way there and back."

"Why don't we hide the bucket and come back for it?" Cyrilla suggested.

They gathered pine needles, moistened them, and covered the bucket with underbrush. The needles would insulate the bucket and keep the water from becoming too hot for their fish. Then Cyrilla took the red ribbon that held her hair back and tied it to a low, overhanging limb. "Now we'll know exactly where to 119 look when we get back," she told the others.

The girls stood back and looked. Satisfied that no one would notice unless they knew what to look for, they hurried on down the path, traveling faster without their load.

As they moved along the path, Ginny Ruth noticed trees hung with strips of linen, some dried and rotted, others still reeking with turpentine.

"The yarb woman's cure to get rid of warts," Beta explained to Ginny Ruth. "Papa once came here for that, although he won't admit it to nobody now."

When they reached the clearing, Evangelina, the yarb woman, was on her knees in a small patch of green plants next to her shack. She was barefoot, and her faded dress hung limply over her body, which seemed more bone than flesh. Her stiff, gray hair straggled from beneath a faded bandanna worn low over her eyebrows.

One eye seemed immobile. The other moved from girl to girl, then back again to the first.

Ginny Ruth shivered, wondering if that was what people meant by "giving the evil eye." She felt the urge to turn and run, and she would have, too, if she'd been alone. But she kept telling herself that there was safety in numbers.

The woman stood, wiping her hands on her dress. She picked up a small basket filled with green sprigs that emitted various smells.

120   "Uh," Alpha mumbled. "Uh."

The woman's eye twitched as she waited impatiently for someone to tell the reason for their visit.

"I need a . . . a potion," Alpha managed to whisper.

"A love potion," Beta corrected, looking anxiously at the woman.

Evangelina gave no sign of caring one way or the other, but she nodded and turned to go inside. The girls stood, looking at one another, and Ginny Ruth wondered if they were supposed to follow her.

Finally Beta, always the bravest of the girls in a crisis, shrugged and stepped inside, leading the others. Reluctantly Ginny Ruth followed them in. The cabin, its only window now in heavy shadow, was so dark that it took her eyes time to adjust.

Evangelina lit a small oil lamp and, replacing the flue, turned to glance at Alpha again. Then she moved to a large shelf at the rear of the room.

Ginny Ruth rubbed her nose to keep from sneezing. The room was musty and smelled of potting soil and drying plants. She didn't see any brimstone, however. She watched as the woman pulled an empty bottle from the shelf, blowing the thick layer of dust from it, then carefully wiping it on the hem of her dress.

Evangelina passed her bony fingers over the assorted bottles, pausing now and then to snatch one from its place and set it on the small table by the window. When she had secured four bottles, each with a different liquid in it, she sat at the table and put two drops of this and a drop of that, four of another into the 121 empty bottle. Each time she held it to the window's light to rotate it, mixing the liquids.

Finally she sniffed, then nodded with satisfaction, gently clutching the bottle to her. She whirled toward Alpha, palm up. Although her meaning was perfectly clear to Ginny Ruth, Alpha stared at it uncomprehendingly.

"Oh!" she said at last, dipping into her pocket to fetch a twenty-five-cent piece for the waiting hand.

Evangelina handed Alpha the bottle, then walked toward the door, as if to dismiss them all.

"But what do I do with it?" Alpha wanted to know. "Put it in his food? Dab it behind my ears?"

"Wear it," Evangelina said. "Around your neck."

"You mean hang the whole bottle there? On a string? What good will that do?" Alpha asked.

Evangelina shrugged. "You believe or you don't. It works or it doesn't. Suit yourself."

Alpha stared at the bottle. "Thank you."

The other girls, hovering together, carefully backed away from the cabin, never taking their eyes off the woman. Alpha followed them, clutching the bottle tightly.

Evangelina dropped to her knees at her herb patch. The girls were already of no concern to her. Ginny Ruth started to leave with the others, but she turned and squatted next to the yarb woman.

"Might you have a potion that . . ." She looked to see if the others were listening. "Oh, never mind."

122

She knew there was no potion in the world that would bring Paw home or stop Mr. Billy's body from being his own worst enemy.

She hurried down the path to join the others.

Alpha breathed a sigh of relief. "Whew! I was *sooooo* scared, I'll tell you!"

"Open it," Cyrilla urged Alpha. "Let's see what the potion smells like."

"Absolutely not!" Alpha told her. "What if whatever good it has could escape?"

"That James had better come through," Cyrilla muttered. "I ain't doin' that no more. It's too scary."

"Just imagine," Ginny Ruth said, dreamily closing her eyes. "A soldier's wife. Why, think of all the places you'd get to go, the different places you'd see." She remembered that Mr. Billy had seen Germany.

Alpha shook her head vigorously. "James'll soon be out of the army. Then he'll be settling down right here to farm with his paw."

Ginny Ruth felt a rush of disappointment. She hoped for Alpha's sake that the potion would fail. Why would anyone deliberately settle for Clemmons?

Beta broke into their conversation. "Look there! I see a bee!"

Since Beta had the sharpest eyes of any of them, the girls looked immediately. None of them could see it.

"Trust her!" Alpha said. "She's never been wrong yet!"

Ignoring the thorns and limbs that snatched at them, 123

the girls half trotted, half loped behind Beta as she bounded off the footpath and through the prickly underbrush.

When she came to a quick halt, the others stacked up against her, unable to stop as quickly. "There! I knew it!" Beta gloated. Sure enough, hanging in the umbrellalike shade of an oak tree was a large honeycomb.

"Why, that's at least three years old. I bet it's got honey galore!" Beta said.

Bees hovered near, darting in and out of its opening.

"And the tree ain't marked. Nobody has found it yet. Come on!" Beta said, skipping toward the tree.

"Watch out!" Ginny Ruth warned. "Those bees'll make honey out of you!"

But Beta was already untying the bandanna from her head and knotting it around one of the tree limbs. Folks were honest enough to honor the claim; no one else would touch it.

Their path to the tree was well marked by snapped twigs and crushed weeds. They'd have no trouble finding their way back to it and home. But Ginny Ruth reminded Beta that bushes would heal quickly, and the path would soon be undetectable. Would they be able to find the bee tree in a month, let alone in the winter?

Beta pulled up her dress, intent on ripping the ruffle
124   from around the bottom of her cotton petticoat.

"Stop!" Cyrilla whined. "That's going to be mine next year."

"Oh, all right!" Beta grumbled. "Then use your ruffle."

"But hers'll be mine!" Daniel said.

Beta sighed. "You're a lot slower growing than Cyrilla. You'll probably have to cut it off anyway. Besides, I'm bigger, and I say so."

Reluctantly Cyrilla ripped the ruffle from around her petticoat. The girls tore it into little narrow strips. As they made their way back toward the footpath, they stopped periodically to tie a strip of cloth to a bush.

"When they die off this winter, we'll have ourselves some tasty honey," Beta told them. "Mmm, just imagine, hotcakes and biscuits topped with fresh honey."

They reached the main footpath. Alpha was still clutching her love potion to her. "Sun's kind of dipping," she told the others. "I didn't think we'd fooled around so long. We better get going. We still got to clean those fish for supper."

"There's my ribbon!" Cyrilla shouted, pointing a few yards ahead.

"Oh, no!" Ginny Ruth shrieked. "Look!" She pointed to the underbrush where they'd disguised their catch. Pine needles were scattered over the path.

Moving closer, Ginny Ruth saw the overturned bucket. Two raccoons were fighting over the last fish and disappeared into the underbrush. 125

The girls stood there helplessly as the dark-ringed tails flicked out of sight. Dejected and hungry, they gathered their fishing gear and started home.

Ginny Ruth made a face, remembering her bragging to the menfolk. She braced herself for the hootings and jeerings that were sure to come.

TEN

The sun was a thin coronet above the tallest of the hills when the girls stepped gingerly over the railroad tracks and crossed the two-lane highway that was Main Street.

Their bare feet slapped against the brick sidewalk. They quickened their steps going past the men and boys who still leaned against the building, socializing.

"Don't you dare brag on what we caught today," Alpha warned the others. "Then we'd have to explain why we don't have those fish. I don't want anybody knowing we were at the yarb woman's."

It was only the fear of reprisal from the Davis girls that kept Ginny Ruth from blurting out the whole story to those who teased them with catcalls and hoots as the bucket swung empty from their hands.

"Don't fret none," Lester called out. "Fishin' is men's work."

"So's gossipin' and loiterin', apparently!" Ginny Ruth snapped.

Lester got the last word with a wink, and Ginny Ruth stalked off, her pole clutched tightly in her hand. **127**

She waved good-bye to the Davis girls, pausing only long enough for Cyrilla to plead with her to help them spy on Alpha and James the next day.

At home Ginny Ruth put her pole on its shelf out back, then went into the cabin to face Maw. "I came back empty-handed," she said. "I'll try again real soon, though."

"Any nibbles?" Maw asked, looking up from stirring the stew.

Ginny Ruth wasn't sure if Maw was really curious or if she was checking up on her. But she decided to squelch the conversation quickly, before the truth sneaked out and she had the Davis clan mad at her.

"Yes'm. I guess I just didn't inherit the fishing knack from Paw. He sure could bring 'em home, couldn't he, Maw?"

Maw sighed heavily, but she didn't answer.

Ginny Ruth, pleased with her maneuvering, decided to go a step further. "We found a bee tree and staked it out, and can I stay in town with the Davises after church to wait for the train to come in? I know I'm supposed to go to Miss Marnie's and read to her a spell, but I can still do that, too, because I know I won't have any schoolwork, okay, Maw?"

In the fading light Maw's face had a softness, a tenderness as she sighed once more, this time with a pleased, faraway look. "Law', I don't see the pleasure in meeting that old train anymore. Now, when I was 128 a girl, that was something else. Back when it stopped right here in Clemmons twice a day, every day, not just special to let someone on or off, back when it still took on whole boxcars of cotton and tomatoes and other vegetables, we'd run down to the depot when we'd hear that whistle blowin'. Didn't matter that we didn't know anyone on the train; it was excitin'. We'd peek into the windows of the dining car. They had crystal and silverware and linen tablecloths and even little vases of flowers on every one of them tables. And the cook— chef, I guess they called him—would smile and wave at us. Sometimes he'd even pass ice out of the little kitchen, if it was real hot. We'd pretend we was a-gettin' on and going to all those glamorous places, like we was a-goin' all the way to New York or Chicago, maybe." Maw smiled and her eyes seemed to dance.

For a brief moment Ginny Ruth saw another Maw, maybe that pretty and saucy young woman who ran away with the handsome "ne'er-do-well."

Then Maw's face tightened back into its more familiar pattern. "Of course, the farmin' died out and the water tower burned and there wasn't no reason for the train to stop here any more. And we'd growed up enough to have some sense in our heads and stop all that foolishness."

Maw straightened her shoulders. "Heaven knows what pleasures you about seeing it these days. It's not the same any more, no sir."

Undaunted, after church on Sunday Ginny Ruth joined the Davis girls out front and hurried with them 129 to the small yellow and brown depot. It was boarded up, and the windows that hadn't been shattered by some local boys trying their skills at slingshots were so dirty as to obscure the inside. They stepped onto the weathered platform, where the train would soon stop with Alpha's sweetie.

Alpha's face flushed with anger when she saw Ginny Ruth, Beta, Cyrilla, and Daniel. "Y'all get on out of here and go home," she yelled. "Y'all are just gonna gawk and giggle, and it's so embarrassing."

The girls moved to the far end of the platform, but that was as far as they intended to go. James's arrival wasn't an event that was to be ignored.

Alpha came down to them. "Please go on back home." Her voice was more whining than demanding now. "Please?"

"Maybe we oughta," Ginny Ruth said. "We don't want to embarrass Alpha."

"The heck we don't!" Cyrilla corrected. "Besides, I want to see if they kiss! She oughta thought about being alone when she went to the yarb woman. She was glad enough to have us along then!"

Alpha's eyes widened as she looked around to see if anyone else was there to hear the reference to the yarb woman. "You're impossible!" she said, tears forming at the edges of her eyes. "You're such . . . such children!"

Alpha moved to the other end of the platform, her
130 eyes shut tight and her lips slightly puckered in a pout.

"I think she's practicing her kissing, don't you?" Beta said, causing the others to dissolve in laughter.

Ginny Ruth bent to touch the track. "I feel it! The track is vibratin'. It'll be here any minute now!" She looked up. "There!" she shouted, pointing. "Just comin' around the bend!"

Alpha paced back and forth, rehearsing her greeting, which turned out to be all in vain. Just seconds before the train arrived James's parents appeared.

"Oh, pooh!" Cyrilla complained. "That spoils everything!"

"We borrowed a truck," his mother said, joining the others on the platform. "We just couldn't bear not to meet James!"

The train squealed to a stop. Steam hissed from its stack and billowed into the air as if it were sighing, impatient to be on its way again. The heat from it made the air look wavery. Ginny Ruth squinted at the windows, where curious faces looked back. A freckle-faced child pressed his nose to the window and made a face at her. She crossed her eyes and stuck out her tongue in his direction, giggling at the shocked look on his face.

James leaped off, struggling with a duffle bag. To everyone's disappointment, mostly to Alpha's, no doubt, James kissed his mother but shook Alpha's hand.

Alpha stood there, her face flushed, clutching the love potion that hung around her neck.

131

Ginny Ruth gawked at James, who'd filled out into a man since his army enlistment. He looked quite handsome in his uniform and as far removed from Clemmons as those houses in the magazine pictures. She wondered whether if Lester left Clemmons he'd come back as presentable as James. She wouldn't miss him all that much if he wanted to give it a try.

James waved toward the girls, shook Alpha's hand again, speaking briefly to her out of everyone's hearing, then left with his parents.

The train whistled mournfully, its call sounding like a lonely coyote. "Bo-ard!" a man in a dark blue suit and visored cap called. The train hissed and lurched forward, off again, its wheels clattering against the track.

Ginny Ruth sighed wistfully as she watched until it disappeared behind the opposite hill, wondering what wonderful, interesting places those passengers would see and just what their destinations were. She smiled slightly, remembering Maw's fantasy about the train. Maybe, deep down, buried so far down that she didn't recognize it herself any more, Maw understood her need to get out of Clemmons.

Satisfied that she'd seen all she was going to see in the continuing saga of Alpha and James, Ginny Ruth waved good-bye to the Davises. She headed home to eat lunch and to get Miss Marnie's poetry book.

Maw was off visiting shut-ins, as was her habit on
132 Sundays. Ginny Ruth ate cornbread and kidney beans,

got out of her pinching sandals, and watered her flowers outside the cabin door. She walked slowly past the Gaithers', but the front door was closed. They were probably out visiting, too.

Scaredy Cat raised his front paws up on the fence and whined until she stopped to scratch his ears. His tail wagged so fiercely it nearly knocked him off balance.

Ginny Ruth giggled. "I'm glad we're still friends, Scaredy Cat," she said. "I hope Mr. Billy is still my friend, too. I'm a terrible person, Scaredy Cat."

She gave the old dog a final pat on the head, then walked toward Miss Marnie's. Her heart quickened as she anticipated the volumes and volumes of other folks' thoughts.

She always looked forward to visiting Miss Marnie. It was like a little bit of heaven to be surrounded by those old books and even the new magazines that showed what the women were wearing in the cities and how they decorated their houses and yards. They were all nestled lovingly on the shelves for her to choose from.

It was nearly five-thirty when Ginny Ruth tapped on the door of Miss Marnie's house, the only two-story in Clemmons. A yellowing coat of white paint still clung to the hard pine lumber as stubbornly as Miss Marnie clung to her own hopes.

Miss Marnie opened the door a crack, then, seeing it was Ginny Ruth, opened it fully to admit her. She 133 was dressed in a challis nightgown and a nightcap tied under her chin, although the hour was still early. "Forgive my appearance, Ginny Ruth, but I'm feeling a bit under the weather," she apologized.

Ginny Ruth smiled to herself. Miss Marnie looked like the granny in Little Red Riding Hood.

"Come on in, dear," Miss Marnie said. "I'll put the kettle on, and you just browse the shelves while I do."

Ginny Ruth strolled up and down the bookshelves, lovingly feeling the spines of the books and the indentations their titles made. Smooth, cool leathers, some stiffly starched linens—each binding held an enchantment of its own. Even the odor fascinated Ginny Ruth. Most of the writers had been dead many years, yet their words lay gift-wrapped there, waiting for someone to read them and be whisked away to other lands and other times. If only she could someday please folks that way.

She pulled out the big, heavy dictionary and flipped through its pages, scanning until she found her favorite word: *tintinnabulation*. She let the sound of it roll around in her head, remembering Edgar Allan Poe's tintinnabulation of the bells, bells, bells. It tasted every bit as good as the orange slices had. She could forgive his keeping her awake nights with his ever-so-scary stories because he'd given her so much enjoyment and beauty, too.

134   And there was *Popocatepetl*. Even if she never lived

to see that snowcapped volcano mountain in Mexico, she would love it forever for the sound of it. Popocatepetl, Popocatepetl.

Her slender fingers flipped back and forth through the pages, letting her eyes scan the dictionary. *Kaleidoscope, in propria persona*—she longed to use them all. How beautiful they were.

"Tea's ready, dear," Miss Marnie called. "Light the lamp for Jake. I'll bring our tea and cookies to the chaise lounge."

Ginny Ruth went to the window facing the tall pines and lit the kerosene lamp, which would burn all night.

Some of the folks spoke in whispers about Jake's disappearance. They claimed to have seen his lantern moving about on foggy nights as Jake's ghost still tried to find its way home. Maw said that was just folks trying to scare their children from venturing too far into the treacherous forest.

Since Jake's disappearance, Miss Marnie had never missed a night of setting that lighted lantern in the window. It must be awful, feeling that somehow she might have caused Jake's losing his way. No wonder she chose to believe that he was still going to come home.

Ginny Ruth squinted, looking out into the woods, half expecting to see a ghostly light tracing a path. All she saw was her own anxious expression in the window. Why couldn't Miss Marnie put that part of her life 135 behind her? With a slight shrug of her shoulders, Ginny Ruth turned away from the window. Dreams die hard; she of all people understood that.

Miss Marnie returned with two bone-china cups filled with steaming, cinnamon-smelling tea. These and a few pieces of sterling silver were her only remnants of a past more glorious than most had known in Clemmons. Miss Marnie was the great-granddaughter of the founder of the town, as well as daughter of the cotton-gin owner.

Her pride was probably even fiercer than most people's. So silently she sold off one piece of Chippendale, then another, to live on. Now she lived in that half-empty house with her pretend grandeur, waiting for a man gone more than twenty years.

Ginny Ruth followed Miss Marnie into the bedroom, where more books lined the walls. In there were the classic tales, which Ginny Ruth thought were as close to poetry as prose ever got. "What would you like to hear, Miss Marnie?" she asked. "Have you something special in mind?"

Miss Marnie settled into the chaise lounge, adjusting her nightgown around her ankles. "You choose, dear. But make it one of the classics tonight. I feel like renewing my acquaintance with an old friend, don't you?"

Ginny Ruth drank in the titles with her eyes. *Ivanhoe, Moby Dick, Tom Sawyer.* She could almost hear

136 the thunder of horses and the clank of swords from

Ivanhoe, the whipping of the wind at sea in *Moby Dick* as she touched the books. Her fingers traveled on down the tight line, stopping at *Arabian Nights*. Yes, that was it: *Arabian Nights*. Sometimes she felt a little like Scheherazade, who told stories to stay alive.

She pulled the book from the shelf and settled at the end of the chaise lounge, adjusting the shade of the lamp to her advantage.

"Before you start, did you light the lamp, dear? Jake will be home soon."

"Yes'm," Ginny Ruth muttered. "Paw, too, I reckon."

As she spoke the words they sounded hollow to her, and she realized something for the first time: Miss Marnie still believed, but Ginny Ruth Grover no longer did.

ELEVEN

Maybe it was the yarb woman's love potion, or maybe it was the natural result of Alpha and James's being reunited. Ginny Ruth couldn't be sure. But, whatever the reason, their plans to marry when James was out of the army in June were made public during the next week's church announcements.

This set off a frenzy of activity traditional to Clemmons. Nimble fingers rummaged through scrap bags all over town, and, under the guiding influence of Miss Alma (and with a certain number of less-than-tactful suggestions from Miss Nettie), a quilt with a double-wedding-ring pattern began to take form at the weekly quilting bee.

Each square of the quilt was made up of thirty-two small scraps, and there were fifty-four such squares. Every woman and girl worked on her own square, which would join all the others in a single quilt top by the June deadline.

Ginny Ruth rather enjoyed the spectacle, spotting and identifying various pieces of cloth. "Why, that's a 138 piece of little Grace's nightie," she told Maw. "And I do believe that that there's Mr. Billy's Sunday best from a long time ago."

The quilts were snatches of everybody's lives, and they were joined to mark the beginning of the new couple's life. Ginny Ruth helped Maw cut enough squares for them each to make a contribution to the quilt. Sad little pieces of cloth seemed to take on new life and radiance as they were combined.

Her threads hopelessly knotted and her fingers bleeding from too-frequent encounters with the working end of her needle, Ginny Ruth finally put her own square in Maw's more capable hands. She concentrated instead on the traditional pounding.

It was the custom for every woman to contribute to the couple bits of what she could spare, often sacrificing more than she could afford in order to make a good showing before her neighbors. Despite its name, it was rarely a pound's worth of anything. But cannisters were set out at a party just before the wedding, or sometimes at the reception after the wedding. Dried beans, flour, salt, sugar, yeast, and cornmeal were put into the appropriate cannisters.

The men participated, too, giving nails, wire, nuts, and bolts. Although these were often practical presents, they seemed to Ginny Ruth silly presents for Alpha and James, because they would live with his family. It wasn't as if they'd be on their own and starting from scratch.

"Ain't she as happy as a dead pig in the sunshine 139

these days?" Cyrilla asked Ginny Ruth as they ate in the lunchroom between classes one school day. "It won't be long now."

Ginny Ruth tried to smile reassuringly at Cyrilla. But she could think only of the hard, rocky piece of land that James's family farmed and the small house that was already too cramped for comfort. Words from her own poem floated through her mind: "crushed beneath some farmer's shoe."

"I do kind of like what happens to the whole town when somebody gets hitched," Ginny Ruth admitted. No matter how beaten down they were personally, no matter how bleak the prospects for the young couple seemed, everyone took on a new zest for life. It was as if they, too, were looking for a fresh start.

Cyrilla motioned toward the cafeteria door, and Ginny Ruth turned to see Miss Alma and Miss Nettie, each trying to squeeze through the doorway at the same time and glaring at the other hard enough to melt her away.

James and Alpha weren't the only two folks in Clemmons with matrimony on their minds. Miss Nettie's plying the preacher with her cooking hadn't melted his heart as yet, and now, to Miss Nettie's pain, Miss Alma had taken up the chase.

Ginny Ruth suppressed a giggle. Miss Nettie was clutching one of her apple pies, steam still rising in little wisps. Miss Alma had a stack of clothing on her 140 arms.

Miss Alma had taken to mending for the reverend—sewing buttons, blind stitching his thinning clothes, and even turning out a pair of muslin cottage curtains for his kitchen window.

"Together they'd make one fine wife," Cyrilla whispered to Ginny Ruth, who finally released the giggle that had been fighting to get out.

"He's always losing a button or snagging his clothes," she told the Davis girls in a whisper. "And since the first Mrs. Trowbridge wasn't all that good a cook, I don't reckon that it'll matter to him in the long run. I'm betting he'll marry Miss Alma and her sewing."

"I don't think so," Cyrilla said. "His stomach has become a lot more important to him now that he's been introduced to real good-tasting stuff. I think he'll marry Miss Nettie and her apple pies."

Ginny Ruth laughed. "He's been nearly fed to death. And practically sewed into his clothes these past weeks. I don't think he wants either of them, really. After school he hardly lets his coattail touch his legs before he's out the door and into his rickety old pickup truck."

The reverend had taken to letting Ginny Ruth and Maw lock up the school in the afternoons. She'd seen him rolling his old truck down the hill to kick the motor over, leaving a cloud of red dust swirling behind it.

That day Ginny Ruth and Cyrilla watched him repeat his routine. "I bet he's going to Iota; his truck turns north every time," Ginny Ruth said.

"I wonder how he gets that old truck started to come back here," Cyrilla wondered aloud. "Iota is at the foot of a hill, you know."

Ginny Ruth put her hand over her heart and made beating motions. "I guess just knowing that his true loves are waiting for him with steaming cobblers and fresh mended shirts gets him all revved up."

At home Ginny Ruth paused at the garden of wild-flowers to admire the profusion of color. She fingered the clusters of bluebonnets with only a slightly sad twinge in her heart as she remembered the poem. "You were kissed by the summer sky," she whispered to the blooms.

Her fingers moved on to the Indian paintbrushes. "And scarlet sunsets are captive in your petals." She felt a poem coming on and hurried inside to write it down before Maw came home and found her "wasting her time."

At supper she told Maw she couldn't in all honesty take any credit for the quilt, since her miserable stitches had to be ripped out and corrected. "I wonder if the flower seeds would make a nice gift instead," she asked aloud. "The flowers will go to seed by then."

Maw ran a biscuit through the gravy on her plate. "Law', with all them young'uns still in the house, I reckon Alpha might wind up eatin' them seeds, instead of plantin' them." Maw clicked her tongue against her teeth.

"Maw, you're terrific! You just gave me a great idea for a present!" Ginny Ruth said. She could hardly wait to tell the Davis siblings the next day.

"Let's get the honey," she told them at school. "It'd be a perfect gift for Alpha and James."

"Are you crazy?" Beta gasped. "It's the wrong time of year. We'll have to wait until winter, when the bees are died out."

"But we can't!" Ginny Ruth argued. "That would be the perfect pounding gift. Nobody else will have anything so fine. Please?" Ginny Ruth begged.

Daniel made a face. "Those bees'll kill us," she said. The others nodded in agreement.

"We'll cover up," Ginny Ruth told them. "We can do it. I know we can. We can divide the wax for candles and the oil for healing. And maybe even keep the older honey that we can squeeze from the combs. We'll give them just the newer, free-flowing honey. Oh, come on. Please?" She showed them her fingers were crossed for good luck.

Ginny Ruth could see that the girls were weakening, so she used her best argument. "I know the menfolks always get the honey. But let's show them we can do it. Remember how they laughed at our fishing?"

Cyrilla's jaw braced against the air stubbornly. "We can do anything they can!"

Beta's shoulders sagged in defeat. "But Ginny Ruth has to take the most chance with the bees."

143

Ginny Ruth spat on her own hand and stuck it out. "If my name goes on top of the giver list," she bargained.

When the girls nodded their agreement, Ginny Ruth wiggled her hand. "Swear?"

Each spat on her hand and slapped Ginny Ruth's hand. "Swear."

The pounding was a few days away, and the girls began to formulate their plans. "Wear a hat and bring sheets of cloth, anything to cover us up," Ginny Ruth told them. She visualized herself covered completely and protected, reaching out with gloved hands to extract the honeycomb that hung among the branches. It seemed easy enough.

After school they met with their supplies, the cloth deftly hidden inside their fish bucket. They carried their fishing poles, figuring it'd be easier to be teased about their fishing prowess than to get everyone into hysterics about their going after a honeycomb at this time of year.

Lester whooped. "Gonna try again, huh? I declare, you girls are just gluttons for wasting your time, ain't you?"

Ginny Ruth poked her nose into the air before he had a chance to wink at her and pranced past him and the others. He'd not be laughing when she came back laden with honey!

The girls carried their bundles along the footpath
toward the bushes that were marked with the fading

petticoat strips. Once they hung back when they heard muttering on the path ahead. They saw Piney, swaying slightly as he followed the trail, talking to himself.

"He's heading for his still, I'll bet," Beta whispered. "He'll be gone in a minute."

When he had moved on, his tuneless song still drifted toward them on the light breeze. The girls spotted the markings and followed them to within a few yards of the beehive.

Ginny Ruth helped the Davis girls tie their sheets around themselves, ghost fashion. Then they did their best, despite their cumbersome wrappings, to cover her. She wrapped her own sheet over her head so that the small tear was just over her right eye, affording her at least a bit of vision.

Ginny Ruth struggled to set a match to the small branch she'd dipped in pitch. Its flame was weak, but it did catch.

"I sure hope you know what you're doing," Beta grumbled to Ginny Ruth.

"Do you know a better way than to smoke those bees out?" Ginny Ruth snapped back. She was tense and scared, and she didn't need any more discouragement than she already felt.

The twigs and bushes reached out to grab at their sheets as the girls crept toward the tree. The Davis sisters seemed to move in slow motion. Ginny Ruth got closer to the honeycomb, the flickering torch in one hand and the metal bucket in the other. **145**

The bees' industrious humming switched to an agitated pitch as they became aware of the impending invasion. The heat from the torch made a few bees drop to the ground, but it also succeeded in making the rest of them more angry.

Beta, who was trembling nearly uncontrollably by now, managed to knock the honeycomb loose so that it fell into the bucket Ginny Ruth held. Then she succumbed totally to the fright that gripped her; she shrieked and ran. Her sisters picked up her panic and ran behind her, shrieking like banshees.

That started a chain reaction among the bees, which swarmed to the nearest invader, namely, Ginny Ruth. Frantically she ran in the direction of the river, trying to ward off the diving bees with her free hand while stubbornly clinging to the bucket of honey.

It was about that time that Ginny Ruth spotted Piney making his way back down the path, a bottle of white lightning tucked under each arm. His bloodshot eyes widened considerably at the sight of the ghostly clan streaking through the underbrush. He seemed sure that they were going after him. Suddenly his own shriek joined theirs in full choral arrangement as he left a trail of shattered glass and splatters of his own special brand of whiskey to run repenting toward town.

The sound of the bees circling her head was nearly deafening to Ginny Ruth. She could feel their sharp 146 stings, even through the sheet. Stumbling over a root that jutted from the path, she managed to recover her balance without falling, but her sheet caught in the brush. As she ran, still clutching the bucket, her sheet was snatched away, exposing her to the wrath of the angry bees.

Ginny Ruth jumped headfirst into the river. She fell in the middle of the screaming Davis sisters. Fortunately the bucket of honey landed in a floating position; Ginny Ruth could see it each time she came up to catch her breath.

Miserably she and the Davises warded off repeated attacks by the bees until dusk finally called them off. It was little consolation that they still had the prized honey.

When she emerged from the river and its soothing coolness, Ginny Ruth realized how swollen and sick she really was. The Davis girls still had their sheets around them and hadn't received nearly the bites she had. Blindly she clutched at the bucket handle and dragged herself from the river, fighting the nausea that swept over her.

She stumbled down the path, whimpering from the pain. Through eyelids swollen half shut she saw a lantern light on the path ahead. As the figure neared her she could see it was Lester.

"There y'all are," he shouted. "I got worried when y'all didn't come back by 'n' decided to come lookin'. What . . ."

Futilely, Ginny Ruth tried to protest when Lester, handing the lantern to Cyrilla, scooped her into his arms and carried her toward town.

Ginny Ruth fought to stay conscious. There was something she had to say. If she was about to meet her maker, she couldn't do it without some last words that counted for something. "Cyrilla," she whispered hoarsely. "Cyrilla, I lied. My paw, he didn't come home Christmas. He never gave me nothing. It was Mr. Billy."

Cyrilla sniffled. "I—I know, Ginny Ruth. It don't matter none. I know'd it already."

Ginny Ruth shook her head, struggling against the void. "Tell . . . tell Mr. Billy . . ."

But everything faded away except the comfort of being carried, of escaping from the pain into unconsciousness.

TWELVE

Ginny Ruth was vaguely aware of the mumble of voices around her. The Davis sisters stumbled alongside, whispering, "Is she all right? Is she gonna die? Oh, please, Ginny Ruth, be all right."

She barely felt Lester's warm breath against her face as he struggled under her weight. He was carrying her home. Home to the cabin. She longed to pull the quilt over her head, to feel the comfort of her own bed. She felt apart from her body, away from its pain. Was death like that? she wondered.

"Good Lord, have mercy!" a woman was shouting. "Ring up Dr. McCaulb in Stallings, then get out to the cabin and get her mama! Quick, boy! Oh, dear Lord, let her be all right. Don't use her to punish a foolish, prideful old woman!"

"Maw?" Ginny Ruth mumbled. "Maw."

"No, child. It ain't your maw. Now, you just lie there. Your maw will come. So will the doctor."

A cool, wet rag touched her face and body. Ginny Ruth whimpered. "I hurt. I hurt so bad."

"The doctor's on his way," a man's voice said. "How is she? Is Polly comin'?"

"I reckon we'll know the answers soon," the woman said.

Ginny Ruth strained to push her swollen lids open, to see who was there and where she was, but she could make out only unfamiliar objects and shadowy figures before slipping into unconsciousness again.

"Ginny Ruth," a familiar voice said. "Ginny Ruth, you have to stay awake, child. Oh, Ginny Ruth, you have to be all right. I couldn't bear—"

"Maw?"

"Yes, child. It's Maw. Talk to me, Ginny Ruth. Stay awake. The doctor is here now. He'll help you."

"Stay here, Maw! Maw, don't leave," Ginny Ruth begged, willing her hand to reach out, despite its pain, to grasp Maw's hand.

Maw held her. She kissed Ginny Ruth's hand. Ginny Ruth felt comforting drops of water spill onto her hand. Tears. She'd never known Maw to cry before, not with everything that had happened.

Ginny Ruth was vaguely aware of the doctor, the shots, the compresses, and soothing, cool baths. She recognized the voices of Maw, Lester, Cyrilla, and Mr. Billy, but whose were those other voices, a man's and a woman's?

When she finally came to, she was swollen and sore, 150 but she felt better. She blinked, looking around. She

hadn't been there before, she knew. There was a crocheted coverlet draped across a small pink chair. On
the wall was a picture of a girl. She looked a lot like
Ginny Ruth, but she was in funny-looking clothes.

Ginny Ruth sat up. "Maw?" she called. "Maw,
where are you?"

Maw hurried into the room. "I'm here, child. Well,
now, don't you look just a whole lot better." She smiled
before tears flooded her eyes and she swooped down
to hug Ginny Ruth more warmly than ever before.

"Oh, my baby! I . . . I was so scared. Oh, thank
God you are all right."

Ginny Ruth sniffled. Maw really did care—a lot.
"Where . . . where are we, Maw?"

"At Mama and Papa's. Lester brought you here. This
was the closest place he could think of. He figured you
were going into shock and needed attention quick.
They called the doctor and sent for me. We've been
here two days, waiting for you to come out of this."

"Mama and Papa? The Simmses?"

"Grandma and Grandpa, child," the woman said,
entering the room. "That is, if you'll call a foolish old
man and woman that, after all these years."

"If my getting stung got me a grandma and
grandpa, then I ain't sorry at all," Ginny Ruth said.
She looked anxiously at Maw. Maw seemed relieved.
So did the Simmses. It was nice not to be invisible
any more.

Mrs. Simms plopped down on the side of the bed. "This here was your maw's room when she was a girl. It looks just like it did then."

Ginny Ruth glanced around, trying to picture Maw as the room's inhabitant. "And that picture up there is Maw?"

Mrs. Simms laughed. "Oh, no, child. That's me!"

Ginny Ruth shook her head in disbelief. Then she did look a lot like the Simmses, after all. It was funny how the eye could deceive you if you wanted it to.

Her grandmother bustled off to prepare some food for Ginny Ruth, who felt she might be able to eat. Maw sat there, holding her hand, looking, just looking at her as if she were seeing her for the first time.

Mr. Simms shuffled in carrying a doll. "We—we saved this all these years. I reckon we waited too long, though, you being as old as you are now. It was your maw's when she was a girl."

Ginny Ruth reached out to take the doll. "It's beautiful. I reckon that nobody ever gets too old to appreciate a beautiful doll. Thank you, . . . Grandpa."

Grandma returned with a tray of coddled eggs and milk toast for Ginny Ruth. "Mr. Billy has been here every day, asking about your health, and I expect he'll be here today, too. He's been just worried sick about you."

Ginny Ruth smiled, realizing that Mr. Billy had forgiven her for her terrible treatment of him. He was 152 a true friend, and she vowed to be worthy of his friendship when she got back on her feet.

Grandma—it seemed surprisingly natural to call Mrs. Simms Grandma—fluffed Ginny Ruth's pillow and fussed about her covers. "Right now you have a couple of visitors," she said, handing Ginny Ruth a shawl to drape around her. She helped her sit up in the bed.

It was Lester and Cyrilla. Cyrilla handed Ginny Ruth her school papers and hugged her.

Ginny Ruth ate as she listened to them tell about school and how Miss Alma and Miss Nettie got into a glaring match when they both showed up to woo the reverend with their domestic charms. They had Ginny Ruth giggling too much to eat.

"Lester," Ginny Ruth said, "was it your idea to bring me here?"

Lester nodded. "I hope it was all right. It just seemed like the right thing to do, under the circumstances. You didn't look like you was faring too well." He grinned. "Besides, you was gettin' a mite heavy to lug all the way out to your maw's place."

"You did right good, Lester, purely you did," Ginny Ruth said. "In fact, I've been thinking. I wouldn't mind at all if sometime you'd like to carry my books home."

Lester looked down at his feet. "Well, to tell the truth, Ginny Ruth, I . . . I done been carrying books for somebody else. Sorry."

"Oh," Ginny Ruth said. "I . . . That's all right, Lester. Really it is."

153

As Lester and Cyrilla started to leave, Cyrilla skittered back and whispered, "Actually, he's quite cute when you get to know him, Ginny Ruth. And so strong!" Giggling, she rushed out of the room to catch up with Lester.

Ginny Ruth felt a pang of indignation. Lester couldn't have been too taken with her womanly charms if he took off the first time she got unconscious! And with her best friend, at that.

Suddenly she sniggered. Ginny Ruth covered her eyes with her hands as she felt a rumbling giggle erupt into out-and-out laughter. Cyrilla and Lester? Would the wonders of this life never cease!

The sharp, jabbing pains disappeared first, then the dull, throbbing ones. Ginny Ruth finally felt like herself again. "I reckon I'm ready to go home," she told Maw. "And back to school."

"Your grandma and grandpa have asked us to move in here, Ginny Ruth," Maw said. "What do you think?"

Ginny Ruth was pleased that Maw was interested in her thoughts. "I'm glad we are a family, Maw. Really I am. And I don't never want to be where we ain't speaking any more. And I want to visit a whole lot now. But home is home. I reckon I'd rather be there."

Maw's shoulders relaxed in obvious relief. Ginny Ruth realized that Maw still cherished her independence, despite the reconciliation. She just wondered

what Maw would have done if she'd wanted to move

in. But she really didn't. After all, she finally understood, she and Maw had made a good home for
themselves.

Before they left Ginny Ruth went around the room,
touching everything there—the quilt, the picture, the
lamp, the scarred bedposts. These were the things from
Maw's other life, and she wanted to know them better,
just as she wanted to know the Simmses better. Clutching her doll to her, she hugged her grandparents, and
then she and Maw walked home.

The wildflowers had spent their blooms and gone to
seed, but somehow the place didn't seem so bad to
her. She had two grandparents, she was nearly free of
the bee miseries, and she'd be due a giant's portion of
gratitude from Alpha and James at the pounding.

Following the regular church services on Sunday,
Alpha and James were married. Alpha wore the veil
from Miss Nettie's hope chest.

The attention paid to them, however, was no more
than that given to Piney, who had combed his hair in
a ragged part, dabbed talcum powder over his un-
washed body, and shown up babbling about seeing
the error of his ways. Between hallelujahs he spoke
incoherently about some white-robed angels who
had come to him in the woods and driven him from
his still.

Ginny Ruth barely stifled a giggle, realizing that she
and the Davises had done what the revenuers had not 155

managed to do in all their years of pursuit. Of course, heavenly apparitions have a way of fading, and no one had reported hearing Piney's still blow up. Somewhere in the shadow of those stately pines, the white lightning still gurgled and dripped slowly into barrels. His conversion probably would last until the new batch of mash was ready.

The services and ceremony at the church were followed by a celebration of dinner on the ground and singing all day in the church yard.

Planks set up on wooden sawhorses and covered with as many tablecloths as the ladies could gather were the gala banquet tables. Everyone brought a covered dish of something or other, mostly beans, since that was what folks had plenty of.

It was all mixed together on the table buffet style, and everybody ate a little of everything. The children chased one another around the trees and under the tables, while the grown-ups looked up from their plates occasionally to shout at them and offer some vague threat.

There seemed to be an extra lot of chatter and buzzing about during this celebration. The reverend had hailed matrimony as the most blessed state and hinted broadly that he might soon be doing "the Lord's will" once again by entering into it himself. Miss Nettie and Miss Alma fluttered about the tables, straightening 156 tablecloths and shooting each other snappy glances, probably each wondering which he'd choose—the cook or the mender.

It was about ten minutes into the dinner when a canary yellow Chevy pulled up on the road. The reverend nearly downed two older churchgoers as he sprinted to reach it.

When he returned to the group, he had a blond, slightly top-heavy young woman in tow, flushing and fanning herself and giggling. Miss Alma and Miss Nettie all but passed out into the potato salad when the Reverend Trowbridge introduced her as Miss Lucy Singer from Iota, his betrothed.

Between eye flutters and fidgeting, she played the role of ninny, revealing that she could neither stitch a dish towel nor boil a potato. It was readily apparent, however, that she could make the reverend hop to and fro, fetching drumsticks of chicken and freshly baked bread, to which she'd contributed not one whit.

It was the first time in months that Ginny Ruth remembered Miss Alma and Miss Nettie speaking to each other. Now they rushed into each other's arms, consoling and complaining and looking down their respective noses at the delicate young thing that "poor Amos" was planning to marry.

Their marital plans shattered and lying about their feet, they migrated to Piney, who grinned and licked his palms to slick down his unruly cowlicks. Obviously he had been chosen as their next project, the realization of which would probably drive him at full speed back to his still.

James and Alpha disappeared during the distractions. Cyrilla—with Lester in tow—whispered to Ginny Ruth that they'd slipped away to have what probably would be their only time alone, since they'd be living with his parents and brothers.

The thought made Ginny Ruth sad again, and she silently promised herself one more time that one day she'd leave Clemmons. The sight of Cyrilla and Lester grinning at each other didn't cheer her much, either.

Those who had cows to milk began to drift from the celebration, leaving the cleaning up to the others. When the tablecloths had been folded and the boards and sawhorses stored in the shed, Maw claimed her bowl and she and Ginny Ruth started home together.

The first stirring of air lifted the red dust at their feet and cooled the sweat beads that had formed over Ginny Ruth's eyebrows and upper lip. She took a deep breath, pausing to look over the land that sloped away from them in every direction.

She could see the unpainted houses and cowsheds, the sparse vegetable gardens, and the zigzag of fences. From there, too, she could see the asphalt highway that sliced through town, the winding dirt road to the cemetery, and the small, narrow footpath home.

An orange and yellow cross-country bus sped down the highway and disappeared behind a stand of pines.

There were people on that bus, maybe even someone her own age, going somewhere, perhaps to a city where horns blared and traffic snarled. Pretending for a moment that she was a passenger, Ginny Ruth watched the bus disappear over the slope.

A cow's long, lowing call returned her attention to the land that stretched in front of her. The delicate fronds of salt grass rustled, making the land look almost like a sea, alive and rippling. She thought about James and Alpha's high hopes, about their mutual love that might not survive the rigors of Clemmons life. "Maw," she said, "did Paw love us?"

"Of course he did, Ginny Ruth," Maw answered, not taking her eyes off the path ahead of her. "Still does, whatever you might think. It's just . . . just he loved his rovin'. He's a wild goose, your paw is. I guess I knew it then, same as now."

Ginny Ruth noticed a smile play across Maw's lips. Her eyes sparkled with a surfacing memory. "Oh, he was handsome, too, your paw was." Her face suddenly clouded. "He just wanted too much outta life, that's all. Just too much."

"What's the harm of wanting some fun, Maw?" Ginny Ruth asked. "Don't you think even the angels like to giggle a little in heaven sometimes?"

"There's no harm in laughter, girl," Maw said. "Law' knows, we did our share of laughing early on. But there comes a time when laughter don't pay the 159 rent and don't buy the baby new shoes. Your paw, he just didn't want to pay the piper ever. And the piper has got to get paid, or the music stops."

Maw shook her head, clicking her tongue against her teeth. "You sound like your paw, girl. It ain't good that you think like him. Mark my words."

"What exactly did Paw want, Maw?"

"Law', girl, I don't know. All I know is he couldn't find it here, couldn't find it with us—with me."

Us? Was that what Maw had said? Us? It had never occurred to Ginny Ruth that Paw didn't want to be with either of them. Maybe a child was as much a handicap as a woman old before her time.

Ginny Ruth stooped to pick a piece of salt grass and suck on it. "But Paw made us laugh and feel good, didn't he, Maw?"

Maw's face softened. "Oh, but he could make me laugh. And feel beautiful and so much alive!" She tightened. "But you can see what that got me, missy. Well, it's the Lord's way of humbling us. We'll just have to make the best of it, that's all."

Ginny Ruth scowled at the red dust that swirled and circled her feet as she trudged home. The Lord didn't have anything to do with her being there. But she, Ginny Ruth Grover, would have something to do with her getting out!

THIRTEEN

Ginny Ruth was more determined than ever to leave the decaying, depressing town of Clemmons. The oppressive heat of the last of spring had withered the gardens but not her spirit. Somehow, eventually, she would visit places that she had only read about in Miss Marnie's magazines and books. Clemmons would be a memory for her notebook.

At the end of the school year, the reverend had said her essays and themes for English were "exceptional." She had taken her report card to the Gaithers'. "It's nice to have a grandpa," she'd told Mr. Billy. "But there just ain't nobody that I can share all my secret thoughts with but you, not even Miss Marnie." Maybe part of it was that she knew he wouldn't go blabbing things she'd said or written to other folks. But a lot of it was the look in his eyes when she recited her poems or read her essays to him. She knew they were truly the kindred spirits she had once called them.

His eyes danced and silently sang when she told him funny, impractical things. And they wept when she shared her sad thoughts. She felt she was expressing 161 what he felt, and wasn't that what writing was all about? Hadn't he said she helped him walk right—inside?

One hot summer day she trotted alongside Mr. Billy, dodging his unsure steps, chattering to fill in the quiet as they headed to the store for Mrs. Gaither. "I got me so much to learn, Mr. Billy," she confided. "But I can't do it here. I have just got to get out, don't you see?"

Mr. Billy muttered, gesturing wildly. But deep in his eyes she saw he did understand.

"I'll be thirteen soon. And then the year after I'll be going to the school in Stallings. But I can't stop there, Mr. Billy. I got to go to college. I got to find out things—like why a rainbow comes only sometimes, and how come the oceans are salty and the river is sweet even though both of 'em are water, and why some folks take what they get without fightin' back, and lots of stuff. And, oh, I gotta get better at my English. I know I got good thoughts most of the time, but folks don't talk like I do in them—those—books. I figure that's gonna cost money, though. And I know I can't count on Maw letting loose o' that cannery money—"

Mr. Billy stopped in his tracks so fast Ginny Ruth nearly ran into him. The scowl in his eyes told her something was wrong. "What's the matter, Mr. Billy? What did I say that was wrong? Maw and her money? Well, that's no never-mind now. I figure I'll just earn my way there, 'cause I'll be thirteen soon, and I figure

I can earn me some travel money, but I gotta find out how much it costs in the city to live and eat and how much the schooling costs and all that stuff."

She took Mr. Billy's arm to steady him as they stepped onto the porch at Ranger's store. The bell jangled as the door shut behind them. Mr. Billy gave his shopping list to Bob Ranger. Ginny Ruth wandered along the narrow aisles, touching the can labels, drinking in their colorful pictures.

"G-G-Gin-ny Ruf," Mr. Billy called, motioning to her.

She hurried over to stand by Mr. Billy. There was a notice on the wall. It was from a farmer about forty miles west of Clemmons who was offering ten dollars a day for cotton pickers. The notice said transportation would be furnished. Anyone who wanted to work should be at the drugstore by 5 A.M. for pickup.

"That ain't much for a day's work, is it?" Mr. Bob said as he stacked the noodles and flour and the wedge of cheese on his counter. "The foreman said the crop's pretty poor, though, and that's all they can afford."

"It sounds like a heap o' money to me, Mr. Bob, purely it does. I'll ask Maw if I can go."

"Har-hard," Mr. Billy said. "H-heat—aw-ful."

"Shoot!" Ginny Ruth said, dismissing it. "It can't be no hotter forty miles west than it is right here. Besides, it's a way out! Don't you see? If I can work just ten days, why, I'll have a hundred dollars. And if I put it in a savings account, by the time I am old 163 enough to leave I'll have . . . well, I'll have more. I don't know how to figure all that percentage stuff."

When Ginny Ruth approached Maw about picking cotton, Maw stared at the palms of her own hands, as if remembering what it was like. "It's a lot harder than you can imagine, Ginny Ruth."

Ginny Ruth squared her jaw. "I ain't—am not—against hard work, Maw. I want that money so I can leave here the first chance I get. I just can't stay here and be like . . . like . . . well, I just can't stay here, that's all. Of course," Ginny Ruth said, "if'n you'd loosen up with your savings some, maybe we wouldn't have to pick cotton."

Maw's mouth was tight. "Missy, why do you force me to tell you things that it ain't right for a girl to know? There ain't no savings. Your paw—he cleaned out that account when he took off." She held up her hand to silence Ginny Ruth. "Oh, don't blame him none, child. He was weak, that's all. He just couldn't help himself. He didn't mean no harm to us, I know that with all my heart." She sighed wearily. "Just weak." She straightened up as if shaking it off. "Well, pick cotton, if you will. It ain't no never-mind to me."

Ginny Ruth's insides felt as if they were on fire. All that time Maw had never once spoken against Paw about the savings. She'd had no idea. How could he do such a thing to his own wife and daughter, leaving them with nothing? Suddenly she understood why their 164 possessions gradually had been sold off and their table had become more and more sparse.

Paw was nothing like Mr. Billy, nothing at all. Ginny Ruth hugged Maw good night, then took herself and her burden of thoughts to bed.

It seemed to Ginny Ruth that she had no sooner fallen asleep than Maw awakened her. Already the smell of biscuits permeated the small cabin. "You need something in your belly if'n you're gonna pick all day," Maw said.

When she was ready to leave for the drugstore, Ginny Ruth was surprised to see Maw coming. "I aim to pick, too," she said. "It ain't like we got plenty of money, you know. Without the school income all summer, it's gonna be rough."

They hadn't been at the drugstore long when a sputtering, lopsided school bus squealed to a stop. The small group of pickers climbed aboard. It took more than an hour to make the trip, with the bus stopping along the way to pick up others.

The first greenish light of dawn was just touching the fields when the bus rumbled to a final stop. Ginny Ruth gazed out at the field, which seemed as if it had been kissed by snow. They wouldn't run out of cotton to pick soon, she reckoned.

A grim-faced man with a barrel chest and a twisted foot passed out tow sacks to each emerging picker. "Take a row and work it to the far end. When you finish that one, start another. When your sack is full, bring it here for emptying."

Maw showed Ginny Ruth how to loop the sack over one shoulder and to work with both hands, feeding it the soft, white blossoms of the plant.

"That's easy," Ginny Ruth said. She snatched at the bolls, dropping them in. She hummed as she picked.

But if Ginny Ruth had thought the harvesting of cotton was going to be an easy way to earn her money, she was soon convinced she'd been wrong.

By ten o'clock her fingers were blistering on the tips. By noon her face and arms were an angry red. The sun was relentless on her head, and her hair felt as if it were on fire.

When the bell clanged for them to break for soup and biscuits, her throat was too parched and her lips too blistered to eat easily. Her temples throbbed like a drum, and she was filled with nausea as the thin soup hit her stomach. Waves of light flashed before her eyes, even when they were shut, and she would have cried if she could have spared the moisture. Her shoulder had been rubbed raw by the sack, and her legs were bleeding from scratches.

She looked at Maw, who appeared to be in no better shape. Yet, when the bell rang for them to return to the fields, Maw was the first to pick up her sack, the first to begin again.

Every step seemed to Ginny Ruth the last she could possibly take. She glanced back over the part of the row she'd already picked clean.

"Don't look back, girl," Maw told her. "You got a

long way to go yet before we leave today."

Maw's face was splotched red and drenched in sweat, but it showed grim determination. Ginny Ruth knew that Maw would give them better than a day's work. They had hired themselves a bargain in her maw, they had. She felt a bit of pride in her and determined to match her boll for boll.

The sun's reflection on the cotton was dizzying. The rows swam before her eyes until she felt her head growing heavy, as if it had swollen.

When they were finally called in from the fields, it was still branding-iron hot. There was a stillness in the air, and breathing came hard. The pickers lined up with their sacks to be weighed, waiting for their pay.

The man with the twisted foot seemed no happier now that the day was done. He tossed Ginny Ruth's sack on the scale. "That ain't enough. You're gonna have to work faster if you expect to get ten dollars," he said, not even looking at her.

Maw tossed her sack on top of Ginny Ruth's. "This is my daughter, and I reckon our sacks together even out just fine," she said. Her mouth was fixed in a determined line.

The man shrugged, handing each of them a ten-dollar bill. "I could bus me up some illegal aliens, you know, that would be happy to work harder and earn less. I ain't gonna make no profit anyway, you know."

"Pah!" Maw said, putting her arm protectively around Ginny Ruth and guiding her toward the bus.

"Thanks," Ginny Ruth whispered.

"You done the best you could," Maw said. "It ain't right to expect you to do a growed woman's work."

Ginny Ruth sank into her seat on the bus. The leather was still burning hot from the sun, but she leaned back anyway, numb to its touch.

The next thing she knew, Maw was shaking her. "Come on, girl. We're home. Wake up."

Home—that was a sick joke. They were far from home. There would still be the long walk from the drugstore. At least the sun had disappeared behind the hills now.

The muscles in Ginny Ruth's legs were stiffening. They fought her every step. Her face was on fire. Even her eyes felt swollen and blistered. It was worse than the bees.

"You oughta had a hat on your head," Maw said, guiding her off the bus and down the path. "You musta come close to having a heat stroke out there. It ain't fit for no child to be working like that out there."

"I ain't—am not—a child anymore, Maw. I'm almost thirteen now."

They heard the squeak of a screen door as they made their way past the Gaithers'. Scaredy Cat romped to the fence line and barked.

Weakly Ginny Ruth held out her hand, wincing as his warm, rough tongue passed over the blisters.

"Get yourselves in here," Mrs. Gaither called. "I got biscuits warming on the stove. And a couple of drumsticks. I know you won't feel like doing any fixin' when you get home. Now, I won't take no argument, you two."

"I can't, Maw," Ginny Ruth said. "I jest can't eat nothing—anything."

But Maw didn't take the time to argue the point. She turned into the gate without a word. Before Ginny Ruth could whimper another protest, she was being attacked by the excited Scaredy Cat.

Numbly she sat at the table while the Gaithers fussed over them. Her eyes kept closing, and she must have fallen asleep several times because she would come to, still trying to chew, and she'd have to remind herself to swallow.

When they had finished eating, Mrs. Gaither scooted them off toward home, refusing Maw's help with the few dishes. Mr. Billy took a small kerosene lantern and insisted on taking them down the dark path home.

Blindly Ginny Ruth stumbled along behind him, sometimes almost running into him as his unsure gait caused him to pause to regain his balance. She fell across her bed, not even remembering if she'd thanked Mr. Billy or Mrs. Gaither for their kindness.

"Wake up, girl," Maw said. "It's time."

Ginny Ruth stirred, sharp pains jabbing at her all over. She whimpered, not bothering to open her eyes.

"Ginny Ruth," Maw said again. "It's time."   169

"I hurt all over," Ginny Ruth said. "It can't be mornin' already."

She remembered nothing more until sunshine warmed her face. Her lids fluttered, struggling to stay open. She pushed herself to her elbows, an awareness rushing into her head with a dizzying effect. "Maw?" she called. "Maw?"

The raucous cry of an angry bluejay outside was her only answer. Ginny Ruth pushed herself from bed. Her ankles were swollen and watery from the blisters. Skin dangled from her lips in dried-out, ragged strips. She swallowed hard, tasting yesterday's dust. "Maw?"

Dipping into the bucket of cool water that sat on the wall shelf, she gently touched it to her face and shivered slightly as it contacted her burning skin.

Ginny Ruth pushed one foot in front of the other, painfully making her way down the footpath toward town. Maybe it wasn't too late, she kept telling herself as she pushed on. But the midmorning sun told her she was wrong.

Dumbly she stood in front of the drugstore where the line for the bus had formed the morning before. Tears welled at the corners of her eyes. A real chance to earn another ten dollars. Ten dollars more toward getting away from Clemmons. And she'd missed it. It was all Maw's fault, she tried to tell herself. Somewhere inside her a little voice was arguing with her, though.

FOURTEEN

While Ginny Ruth was staring at the spot where the bus had been the morning before, the screen door to the hardware store whooshed shut, and the Gaithers came out. Mrs. Gaither clutched a parcel to her. "Why, Ginny Ruth, whatever are you doing here this time of morning, child? I thought you wuz workin' in the fields!"

A low moan erupted from deep inside Ginny Ruth. "Maw didn't get me— That is, I didn't get myself up in time, Mrs. Gaither, and I wanted to earn that money so bad, purely I did. But I just hurt all over."

"Of course you do, child," Mrs. Gaither said, clucking over Ginny Ruth like a mother hen. "But those are just growin' pains, darling. Growin' pains, that's all." She put her arm around Ginny Ruth's shoulders and guided her down the dusty red path from town.

Ginny Ruth glanced at Mrs. Gaither out of the corner of her eye. What she was suffering from were working pains, plain and simple. What did Mrs. Gaither mean, growing pains?

"Your—maw?" Mr. Billy said. "F-f-fields?"

"Poor Maw," Ginny Ruth said, a sudden fit of guilt engulfing her as she remembered how Maw had felt last night. "Maw went back, and I know she was as tired and as pained as I was. You should've seen her taking up for me with that foreman! He was mad at me 'cause I didn't get as much cotton as the rest of 'em."

"Well," Mrs. Gaither said, "just 'cause your body ain't got the strength of a woman yet don't mean your head's waitin' for it to catch up, child. You can think things through, all right. For now you come on in and have something to eat. We still got some biscuits in the keep, and some syrup, and I might even scare up a cut o' bacon for you."

Ginny Ruth felt like a kicked puppy. There wasn't a spot on her that didn't ache more than she'd ever ached in her life. Numbly she sat at the Gaithers' table and forced herself to eat. What would Maw be having for her lunch at that old cotton field? More of that watered-down soup? She scowled. How come Maw had to be so strong and work like an old ox? It made her feel guilty. She didn't like feeling guilty, feeling she was falling as far short of Maw's expectations as Paw had. She sniffled. "I feel so . . . so confused right now. I'm mad at Paw because he ain't never coming back. I'm mad at Maw because she is so . . . so strong. And I'm mad at me 'cause I ain't like neither of 'em."

Mr. Billy's eyes seemed to spill over. He pushed 172 from the table and hurried back, shakily clutching a tablet of paper and a pencil. He shoved them at her. "B-both," he mumbled. "Both."

She looked into his liquid blue eyes and saw herself reflected there. Then she understood. She held the pencil poised over the paper, biting her ragged lip in thought. Suddenly she wrote:

> *Paw is a wild goose who rides on the wind.*
> *Maw is an ox, strong but hardened to*
> *   the bit.*
> *But who am I?*
> *Am I him?*
> *Am I her?*
> *Am I neither one?*

She frowned, remembering what the reverend had said. She rewrote:

> *Am I he?*
> *Am I she?*
> *Am I neither one?*
> *I am both.*
> *Mostly I am me.*

She folded up the paper and put it in her pocket, thanking Mr. Billy. "I'm going to be in that field tomorrow, Mr. Billy, even if I have to sleep in front of the drugstore tonight. I'm gonna earn myself some money for schooling somewhere else, purely I am. But for today, I know what I got to do."

Ginny Ruth hurried to Ranger's store. If she really   173

was like both of them, she would let Maw's strength and determination take her through the cotton-picking tomorrow. But for today she would gladly accept the impractical Paw side of herself. She had Mr. Bob sell her half a stewing hen and a half pound of green beans and a stick of butter.

Proudly she pulled out the ten-dollar bill, pleased with Mr. Bob's expression when she offered cash instead of charging the purchases.

She hurried along the path home, waving at Mr. Billy, who was puttering in his front yard when she passed. "Thank you, Mr. Billy!" she called. "I am both, and I'm glad!"

By the time Maw came in, Ginny Ruth had stewed chicken, buttered baked potatoes, and green beans ready.

"Good Lord have mercy!" Maw exclaimed. "Where did you get this banquet?"

Ginny Ruth squared her shoulders. "I paid cash for it and I still got me more than five dollars left to start a bank account with. And when I'm finished working this summer, I'll have me a tidy start toward school somewhere else."

Maw clicked her tongue against her teeth. "That was highly impractical of you, Ginny Ruth, to spend so much on a meal that will be only a memory tomorrow. Sometimes you are as bad as your paw."

"There ain't—isn't—anything wrong with that, 174 Maw. There isn't anything wrong with being happy."

Maw stared into an empty corner, sighing slightly. "Maybe you are right, Ginny Ruth. Maybe if I hadn't been so hard on your paw . . . " Her voice trailed away, leaving the thought hovering in the air like a specter.

She didn't even protest when Ginny Ruth hustled her off to bed early and did the dishes herself. "But don't forget to wake me in the morning, Maw," Ginny Ruth said. "And if I don't respond, throw a dipper of water on me. I intend to go, even if I have to walk all the way."

As it turned out, Ginny Ruth was the first one up the next day and all the days after that. She was determined to up her harvest each day.

The days melted into weeks, and, when the cotton was done, they picked tomatoes. Ginny Ruth slid the money she'd earned into her notebook each evening.

"You'll be thirteen in a few weeks," Maw said. "You can open your own account then."

When her birthday finally arrived, Maw said, "Maybe we shouldn't work today, being it's your birthday."

"I reckon it'll still be my birthday come sundown, and I won't be doin' anything special for the occasion anyway. Cyrilla's so caught up with Lester I hear she don't have time for anyone anymore. Besides, that'll be ten dollars more when I—"

"Ginny Ruth!" Maw said. "I don't intend to go picking today, and I don't want you to. That is, I think you should go into town and set up your bank account." 175

Ginny Ruth frowned, thinking. That seemed awfully impractical of Maw. Then she realized that if the money was in the account, it could be earning some interest, which it couldn't do nestled in her notebook. It really wasn't practical to wait until the crops were all in.

They tidied up the cabin and weeded their small garden, then left for town around eleven.

When they were near the Gaithers', Maw said, "Let's stop in a minute."

Ginny Ruth twitched with excitement about her account. "Can't we do that on the way back?"

"I think we should do it right now," Maw said, leaving no question as to whose will would prevail.

Scaredy Cat bounded up, licking Ginny Ruth eagerly. The three of them climbed the front steps.

Mr. Billy opened the door, greeting them. "Ha-hap-py bir-day."

Ginny Ruth hugged him. "Why, thank y—" She looked up to see Miss Marnie and the Simmses standing with Mrs. Gaither, smiling at her. "Why, Miss Marnie! Grandma and Grandpa! I'm glad y'all happen to be here at the same time."

Mrs. Gaither laughed. "Why, child, this ain't no happenstance! This here is a birthday party!"

The Simmses gave Ginny Ruth a winter coat. Ginny Ruth slipped into it, dazed. "Y'all shouldn't 'a' spent so much on me!" she squealed, although secretly she was glad they had.

"We got it on sale—half price," Mr. Simms said.

Ginny Ruth grinned, realizing where Maw got some of her practicality.

"Well, when you think of all those birthdays of our only grandchild we missed, it is a small price," Mrs. Simms added.

Mr. Billy struggled to hand Ginny Ruth something. It was a package containing ten red pencils with her own name printed on them in gold letters and a new notebook.

"Oh, thank you, Mr. Billy!" Ginny Ruth said. "I reckon I will fill it up right fast."

Miss Marnie gave Ginny Ruth a dictionary. Ginny Ruth hugged each of them, grateful.

Then Mrs. Gaither brought in a package. It was the same brown-wrapped parcel Ginny Ruth had seen her with weeks ago. She handed it to Maw.

Maw stared at her feet, then shoved it toward Ginny Ruth. "Happy birthday, Ginny Ruth. I ain't said this much, but I'm proud of you, missy."

Ginny Ruth stared at the parcel. It was addressed to Maw. Mrs. Gaither must have been holding it for her all that time. She saw the return address was Sears.

Ripping into the package, Ginny Ruth gasped. "A store-bought dress! Oh, Maw! And—and shoes!" Tears flooded her eyes as she hugged Maw. "A real store-bought dress! Maw, that is so wonderfully impractical!"

Maw cleared her throat, clicking her tongue against her teeth. "Not at all. I . . . I don't have time to be 177 making dresses for a girl that's gonna grow clean out of 'em."

Ginny Ruth giggled, but she didn't say anything. Let Maw pretend she was as practical as always, if it pleased her!

"Come on back in the kitchen, now," Mrs. Gaither said. "I got us some home-cranked ice cream and a big old cake."

Ginny Ruth lovingly folded her dress into the package and started to follow the others, but Maw held her back. "Jest this one other thing, Ginny Ruth. This here is yours, too. When you add yours to it, it'll be a pretty tidy sum. And Mr. Billy's been doing some checking for me. When the time comes for you to go to college, you can work your way through, and he figures you might even be good enough to get one of them—uh, them scholarships. He said that ain't charity; that's a reward for being smart."

Ginny Ruth stared at the bank book with her own name on it. It already had three hundred dollars listed. "Your money, Maw? You been working so hard all summer and you are giving the money to me? Why?"

Maw rubbed her calloused hands together nervously. "I don't really understand your need to fool around with fancy words no more than I ever understood your paw and his flights of fancy. But I ain't the fool twice over. I want to help you get your dream."

"I understand a lot more now, Maw, than I did just 178 a few months ago. I'm proud that I found a bit of your practical nature hiding down deep inside me. I admit it needs coaxing and nurturing, and I am gonna need your help with that. But without that practical side that is making me work for what I want, I would be just a dreamy-eyed girl, writing unread poetry all my life. I'd be just like Paw, chasing dreams over the next hill."

Ginny Ruth wiped away a tear that had spilled onto her cheek, then added, "But, Maw, I hope you don't mind if I keep a bit of that part of Paw, too. It gives me such a good feeling."

Maw threw both arms around Ginny Ruth and hugged her tight.

Ginny Ruth knew she could do it alone if she had to, but she was warmed, knowing that Maw was helping.

"Y'all come on!" Mrs. Gaither called. "The ice cream's a-meltin'."

"You go on, Maw," Ginny Ruth said, grinning. "I'll be right there." She grabbed one of her new pencils and her notebook. Ginny Ruth Grover felt a poem coming on.